Where's Kazu?

the Maison de Danse Quartet

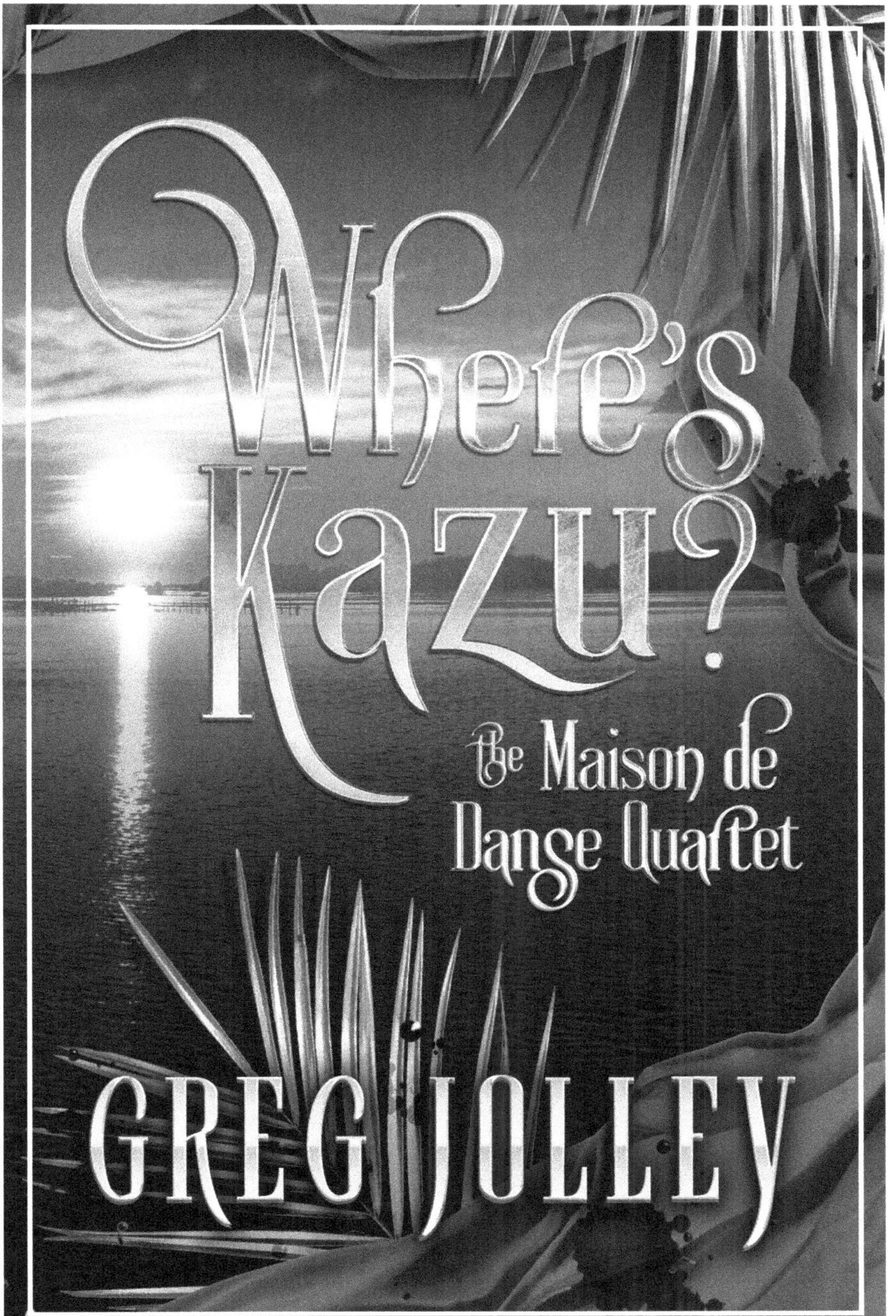
Where's Kazu?
The Maison de Danse Quartet
GREG JOLLEY

WHERE'S KAZU?
BOOK ONE OF THE MAISON DE DANSE QUARTET

Published by Épouvantail Books, LLC.

ISBN-13: 978-1-0880-0086-1 (Hardcover)
ISBN-13: 978-1-0880-0074-8 (Trade Paperback)
ISBN-13: 978-1-0880-0080-9 (Ebook)

For information, write:
Épouvantail Books, LLC
226 North Nova Road, Number 381
Ormond Beach, FL, 32174

Visit the publisher: https://épouvantail.com

Cover design: Fay Lane

First Edition

Dedicated to Bob and Elizabeth Randall,
an important and brilliant team telling great stories

Thank you

Thomas Berger
The fine skeletal prose of Elmore Leonard
Flagler Beach, Florida
Villa Serano
Buck's Gun Rack, Daytona Beach

Part One

Windmill

You miss one hundred percent of the shots you don't take.

~ Lee Harvey Oswald

Chapter One

Jappy

My life orbited around Wednesdays when the crime-splattered newspapers arrived from Mexico.

Sickening graphic photographs under screaming headlines in blood red. The gunshot victims on the sides of nameless roads. Men, women, and children dismembered by explosives or machetes. I waded into the five newspapers each week, all from the west coast of Mexico, the vacation paradise of tourists and high-rise hotels, swimming pools, swim-up bars, seven meals a day, and free-flowing alcohol.

Five penniless farmworkers who had unloaded the wrong truck had their eyes gouged out with a fork before their tongues were sliced off and two bullets were pumped into their foreheads. Close-up facial images of the five were included. In color, of course. There were stories about tourist kidnappings, murders, gunfights, and drugs streaming in the gutters. Good old festive, tropical Puerto Mita.

Opening my dog-eared English-Spanish translation book, I waded in. Like every Wednesday, with Rhonda's help, I was looking for clues.

At the top of page two was a lurid headline sprawled sideways across the photograph of a rental car riddled with bullets, two bodies spilling out into the dust from the left side doors. Page three featured the breathless story and images of a suspicious beachfront hotel fire, complete with a middle-of-the-night gunfight, leaving two employees and a guest under white sheets. On the bottom of the page, Rhonda had placed one of those silly red plastic arrows. The *Puerto Mita Crónica* had relegated the latest news off to the corner. I read the headline.

"La Caza de Jappy el Niño Asesino!"

Let me translate that: "The Hunt for Jappy the Child Assassin!" written by some hack ex-patriot named Carson Staines. I'd read his articles before. He clearly had Jappy as a bone he refused to bury, still chewing for scraps of grilse.

The article was a rehash, nothing new, deserving its continued slide to the rear of the *Puerto Mita Crónica*.

No new photographs. One repeated description from a witness of the airport killing three weeks prior. Obviously worked up for drama by Mr. Staines.

"A handsome Asian boy, calm, cleverly disappearing by melting into the panicked crowd, acting just like them, all tears of fears."

The "calm and clever" description resonated, ringing the bell, awakening memories I had of the boy, *if* it was the same child I had last seen over two years ago. Not a lot to go on, as many twelve-year-olds have those qualities. But how many cool and resourceful "Asian" boys were running the back streets of Puerto Mita?

The only known photograph of Jappy was taken by the same Carson Staines, an unfortunate shot of the boy's back. The boy was wearing black boots and shorts in the photograph and his hair was long and black. It's what was in his left hand that sparked Rhonda and me down this rabbit burrow of questions and digging.

The hat was a worn black baseball cap. It was turned in his hand, so only a curve of gold showed, like the round of a fishhook. Could it part of the letter P? I believed so. Rhonda was still on the fence, but as always, more than willing to help.

"If he lived through that plane crash, how has he survived?" she only asked once, since I had no idea.

Here's what I knew. There were two flights; both headed to the southern seaside la Diana resort. His parents, Bill and Ali, and the luggage were in one of the Cessna's. The boy and his pal were in the second small aircraft. The first airplane made the short trip with no problem. The other Cessna turned and headed north. Why the airplane headed in that direction, no one knows. The weather was clear. There were no distress calls.

The four-seated airplane crashed in the jungle fifty miles north of Puerto Mita. A search was carried out. The wreckage was found a week later. There were no survivors. Some remains were found. Animals had been at them. That's what happens in the jungle when planes crash.

Assuming he lived through the plane crash, how could a farm boy from Kansas survive in that country for this long?

It pained my heart to think of him somehow climbing from the jungle and, against all odds, finding a village or town, probably injured, not knowing the language.

"If it is him, why didn't he make calls, go to the police?" Rhonda asked once. I had no answer. We agreed to set aside that piece of the puzzle. The most vital clue we had was that black hat with what looked like the backside of a golden letter P.

I put aside the other four newspapers. There were no tiny red arrows on their pages. Like every Wednesday, they had arrived bound with a creamy-yellow silk bow. The bow made the package resemble a birthday gift. All the more because Rhonda always included a card in the same buttery hue when she sent the papers to me.

I slid the envelope from under the bow. Opening it on top of the remaining newspaper, I took out that week's write-up on stationery in a strictly business font.

December 17th

Pierce A. Danser
Jeep Dealership of Dent
1301 Whitmore Lake Road
Dent, MI 48189

Hello Pierce,

I hope this finds you blah blah blah.

No new news is, well, no new news.

This week I reached out to that writer, Carson Staines. No reply (yet) to the three requests. My next step is bribery. Surely, a newspaper hack trying to make it by working for that dusty country's newspapers could use an envelope of US cash.

So far, the Federales down there are playing all nice-nice with me. So concerned, so sincere, so not sharing dick. I have a call into the prosecutor's office and follow-up letters to him and the chief of the Puerto Mito police.

Odds? They will dance and romance us with empathy, giving us nothing new. I'll transfer funds from your account with your permission, hoping that offering them fat envelopes might open their files and memories.

I'm still convinced that our best source will be that Staines guy. He was on the boy's tail aggressively, doing that series on him.

Below was more on the *other* topic she and I were working on.

> Your wife has telegrammed again about the papers. As always, polite and gracious. Her lawyer has tried to speak with yours. That, of course, was a waste of time. Do you even know where he is? A second set of papers is headed your way. Rubbing in just a bit of salt, I did advise you to never hire a lawyer who has his face pasted on a billboard.
>
> Enough on that.
>
> This coming week I'll work on all I said I would in the above. I'm confident we can crack Staines open like a coconut.
>
> Have you even looked at that film offer? The working title is "Death Can be Murder," and it would get you back in the cinematographer's chair.
>
> Here's wishing you a fine week in that frozen tundra.
>
> Rhonda

Rhonda and I worked together a few years back at the Blue Wave movie studio. She was a continuity editor also assigned to research and fact verification. Her smarts, creativity, and high energy advanced her up the ladder from when she was a star minder, assigned to my wife, Pauline Place. Yes, *that* Pauline Place, the renowned actress, but you know that. In those days, I was considered a crackerjack cinematographer. Nowadays, I sell Willys, but more on that later, if at all.

I folded the letter back inside the envelope and that went into the top drawer of my desk: nothing else in there but the prior ones.

Looking out the plate glass windows, there was winter in all its sleety, icy, snowy, cold. My thoughts turned to the boy in sun-fried Mexico.

I could probably afford the proposed bribes of that writer and the Mexican officials. The question was, how far do I want to run with this vague quixotic puzzle?

The last time I talked to my soon-to-be ex-wife, we discussed what I knew and didn't know and what I was thinking—hoping, really. Pauline thought I was chasing ghosts again. I can see her shaking her head with a beautiful and complicated expression; this one a blend of sincere sympathy and wry sadness at my latest antics.

Out in the Michigan winter, the mail truck pulled in, struggling up the driveway past the four Willys on display out front of the dealership.

Music played from within the stir on my desk, a Steely Dan jingle. I found my iPhone in the paper riot to my right.

It was Rhonda.

"Hey ya, Pie. That Staines creep left a message. He's *very important*, just so ya know. And as expected, a greedy mother-lover. The skag-sack is open to negotiations. Wants ta talk money before anything. Not even a crumb before." Rhonda had dusted off her Dixie-Chick accent. She enjoyed playing with them for her own reasons.

Outside, the mailman slipped on the ice and nearly tumbled, coming up red-faced angry.

"Whatcha thinkin?" Rhonda asked. "Wanna see how much he's asking fer? I can set up a call with him. Get his initial laughable amount, insist on some *crumbs* first, of course."

The mailman was cursing and struggling with the sliding glass door. I was stalling to phrase my reply.

"Is this another one of my foolish pursuits?" I finally asked.

"Likely, but a good one. Perhaps even admirable."

"I want to see that twelve-year-old killer's face."

"It's likely. Our Carson Staines also advertises himself as a photojournalist. Has his own website, of course."

"If you would, talk to him, please. I'll join the call if you like."

She responded with twangy laughter.

"Leave this to me, please. Don't need you tryin' ta reach through the phone line to strangle him."

"Right, yes. Thank you. And Rhonda?"

"Yes?"

"What is a skag sack?"

"I'll draw one for you sometime. "How're the Jeep sales?"

"*Willy* sales. None, of course."

Tapping my wedding ring on the desk, I watched the mailman stomp his boots on the pristine showroom tiles. He was arguing with himself.

"You realize that now *we're* more than just nosing around," Rhonda drawing the "we're" out like a slow-rolling river.

"The boy, this Jappy the Killer as they call him," I asked. "You think it could be him?"

"I think it could be him."

"Start the talks, please. Send me whatever you can get out of this…" I paused, digging up an ill-born attempt at a Southern accident, "pho-ta jour-na-list."

"Gladly, I love crushing cockroaches. Whatcha gonna do?"

"What I always do when ma head's a spin."

"Tell him howdy for me." Rhonda ended the call with a soft purr of Southern mirth.

I needed to get some perspective. To lean on a mind much smarter and creative than my own. And who better to go to for advice than a washed-up, once-famous actor, current auto mechanic and grease monkey?

Chapter Two

Dot & Walton

The mailman was either morning drunk or miserably hungover. His face was disfigured by alcohol: blotted, veined cheeks and nose, with red, wet eyes down. There were three days of stubble on his weak chin.

"Here's-the-mail," he said as one word, answering the question: his breakfast had been a few cups of clear coffee over ice.

He carried a roughed-up white tub of mail in red, trembling hands. I followed him over to Sam Say's office. He's the current general manager I hired a few months back. Sam's real last name is Szczepanski, which is why I call him Sam Says. His office is in the center of the dealership, and like mine, a square glass fish tank.

The mailman set the tub on the corner of Sam's desk, not looking up, his tortured eyes to the floor. Sam didn't look up, either. He was busy on his large-screen computer. He spent his 10 a.m. to 5 p.m. shift in the worlds of video games and something called Reddit. I didn't mind. If we ever got a customer, he was there to do the talking. The dealership was new and immaculate and the smallest in the United States. There are the four Jeeps out front and the fifth in the middle of the showroom. All five are brand new and white. All five are the Willy model.

Stepping into Sam's office, I waited until the drunk and his mail tub left for the day. My general manager was too preoccupied to give me or the mail a glance, so I went through it. There was the usual flotsam of power and gas bills, advertisements, and another of the letters from the Jeep-Chrysler Corporation. These typically carry veiled threats. You could say our sales performance was underperforming. There was one odd letter, addressed to me in handwriting, with foreign stamps on the battered envelop. Pocketing that one, I set aside the rest of the mail for Sam Says to go through later, if at all.

"I'm heading out. Get the door for me?" I asked.

Sam looked up at me like he just realized I was in his office.

"Sup?" he asked.

"Get the door for me?" I repeated.

The request caused him obvious pain. His fingers came off the keypad slowly, reluctantly.

"Sure, boss. Gimme a second."

I left him still looking at his monitor with transfixed, dead eyes. We kept the lockbox of Jeep keys in my office. By the time I climbed into the showroom Willy, Sam was at the left side wall, pressing the control button that raised the door to the parking lot. I started the Willy and rolled across the polished floor. A two-foot rise of hard-packed snow had formed against the outside of the door and I crunched through it, leaving the warmth and brilliant lights of the showroom behind.

December was in all its Michigan glory. A world frozen white under constantly dreary, gray skies. After plowing ten yards out, I braked and put the transmission in four-wheel drive and low range. I knew I had asked Sam to arrange to have the dealership's parking lot snow plowed. Shame he was so overworked.

I turned left onto Whitmore Lake Road and headed south in the direction of Ann Arbor. With the Willy in low range, I crept along like a senile geriatric, and I was good with that. All this living in a winter wonderland was still new to me.

The trees alongside the two-lane were heavy with snow, as were the few roofs of tiny houses along the way. Cranking the heat control to high, I focused on keeping the daytime headlight beams centered in the narrow, iced tunnel carved through the drifts. The town's snowplows must have made a pass some hours earlier, but fresh falling snow stood nearly two feet deep. The wipers sweeping, the big tires hushing, I was a mile along when a pickup truck pulled out from a side street. I was pleased at first, letting it carve tire furrows I could follow in.

A Confederate flag was unfurled from a pole in the truck's bed, a fine symbol of idiocy. I followed this rim job, wishing he would hit a rut, swerve, slide and plow into a tree. But not before he cleared the way to my turnoff.

At the Barker Road intersection, the truck carried on across. I turned right, feeling the four-wheel-drive gripping solid through the steering wheel.

Barker Road looked like it hadn't been plowed in days. It was one of the many backroads not deemed worthy. Snow began climbing the hood and brush the sides of the Willy. Keeping the fine and heavy vehicle at a grandfatherly ten miles an hour, I drove down the center of the road for the next three miles.

The first sign of civilization was a long-ago shuttered Sunoco gas station to the right. A hundred yards farther along was Whitmore Antiques, the shop in a former residence of red brick; a single light was on in a side window. The antique shop was nearly buried in white. Vacant lots passed along both sides for the next half-mile. The start of a high fence appeared to the right, the first sign of my destination. I put the blinkers on for no reason I can think of and pulled into the parking lot of Gustin's Packard Restorations.

The office was at the front of the large warehouse building. Its windows were dark, which was the norm. People out shopping in a snowstorm for Packard parts are as rare as those desiring new white Willys. Besides, all the action was inside the warehouse, where my best friend and the owner and three mechanics spent their workdays rebuilding the once famed cars from the rows and aisles of spare parts on pallets.

I steered for the second gate to the left side, past the three-story building. That was where Ryan Dot lived. Yes, *that* Ryan Dot, the former over-the-top famous actor. He was currently employed at Gustin's Packard Restorations, where he found true meaning and satisfaction restoring the once-grand automobiles.

Beyond the gate was the small front yard, deep with snow, and his twenty-three-foot rebuild Airstream trailer. There were two Airstreams in the yard, facing each other, the second belonging to Walton, his long-time difficult and adored girlfriend.

I parked and climbed out into knee-deep snow. The miserable and frigid late morning air gripped me.

"Uh oh," the two words formed a cloud. There were no fresh footprints between the two trailers—a clear indication of that week's status of Dot and Walton's hot and cold relationship. There were footprints to his Airstream. And a second pair of footsteps to her trailer. Both sets coming from the side door to the warehouse.

I crossed and knocked on Dot's door.

"Come on in, whoever you are," carried from inside.

Finding my footing on the steel step, I climbed and entered.

"Compadre," Ryan Dot greeted me, leaning from the ridiculously tight kitchenette. There was his famous and handsome face, often described as beautiful: a fine, thin nose, mischievous and alert blue eyes, black curly hair cut short.

"Smells like heaven in here," I replied.

Dot was wearing an apron and oven mitts. The air was rich with cinnamon buns warming in the oven and the beautiful scent of his Mr. Coffee filled with espresso.

"Taking an early lunch break. We started at five this morning on a '49 Custom Eight Sedan. Some buyer in Vegas has to have it shipped by next Tuesday. Have a seat. Unload your worries. You're looking your usual perplexed."

"Thank you." I sat at the table, which could be removed to fold out a bed if Dot ever decided to have company. A newspaper was laid out and an ancient carburetor was half dissected on it. Other than that, his home was spotless.

"How have you been?" I asked.

"Good. Interested. Join me?" he held up the pie pan with the buns.

"Coffee, please."

Dot set the cinnamon buns on the table and poured each of us a small cup of espresso. He handed me one and sipped from the other. Neither of us ever added sugar. He sat down opposite me.

"And?" he asked with his ready, winning smile of perfect white teeth. "No. Let me guess. You've decided that the dealership might not have been the best life choice?"

"Constantly," I grinned.

"You've been content with that for what, a year and some? A good choice, but… you fill in the next part."

"Yes, but…" I watched him take his first delighted bite. I took a sip of coffee.

"Rhonda and I are close to certain."

"How close to certain?

"Close enough for action? That's where I'm stuck."

"And?"

"And… Am I chasing windmills again?"

"Probably, but a good one to chase."

The trailer door opened, followed by a knock. There stood Walton, a bouquet of yellow lilies in hand, looking to Dot, head tilted, eyes hopeful.

"Hey, Pie," she said to me, her gaze never leaving Dot's.

Dot stood from the table.

"How's our favorite Walton?" I asked.

"I'll know in a minute."

I watched the two of them. Dot, the former movie darling. Walton, all wholesome Midwestern beautiful, her skin a fine caramel, even in winter. She formed a sideways, loopy smile, her lovely eyes intense, studying Dot.

"I say we put a stake in the argument." She offered him the flowers.

"I'll get my mallet." He took the lilies and smelled them.

She leaned. So did he, and they kissed.

As Dot got a pitcher from the tiny kitchen and put the flowers in it, Walton nudged me with her hip and scooted in beside me. She chose a bun from the pie pan.

"How's my favorite car salesman?" she chewed.

"Befuddled."

"As always," she smiled and kissed my cheek with sugary lips, taking the edge off the "As always."

Dot sat down across from us and selected a second bun.

"Pie and Rhonda have made progress," he told Walton, "By the way," he turned to me, "any new photographs of him?"

"No, but Rhonda's on that. There's this journalist."

"An expensive one?" Dot had a good amount of experience with hushing reporters and paparazzi.

"That's my bet. She's working that, too."

"The amazing Rhonda," Dot reached across and took Walton's hand.

"So, what's the next step? Your next step?" Walton asked and raised Dot's hand and kissed it, her curious eyes turning to me.

"That's why I'm here," I smiled at the two of them.

"Need a nudge or another boot on the brakes?" she asked.

"Exactly."

Dot laughed. "*Exactly* isn't a decision."

"I'll add you to my prayer list," Walton chimed. "Mail it off to god. She's so skippy awesome."

“Thank you.”

“It’s a good quest. Nice and improbable,” Dot went with the nudge. “My opinion? Book the flight.”

“But, gee, Pie, can the smallest Jeep dealership in the country survive without you at the helm?” Walton asked, tongue in cheek.

All three of us smiled at that.

“Dot, thank you. Both of you,” I nodded to Walton, “I’m closer to deciding. Let me see what Rhonda comes up with in the next twenty-four hours.”

“If you go, please be careful,” Walton took a sip of Dot’s espresso and closed her eyes in pleasure. “Yum,” she purred.

“You two will play nice-nice while I’m away, if I go?” I asked.

“Except when we’re brawling, of course.” Dot has always had a fine pirate’s smile.

Walton stood and circled the table and slid in beside Dot. I looked at Dot’s handiwork with the carburetor on the table before I stood.

“Thank you, both.” I started to the kitchen to rinse out my coffee cup.

“De nada, you will be going with god,” Walton offered.

“You get in a bind, you call,” Dot said.

“Will do, *if* I go.”

“You’ll go,” Dot encouraged. “How can you not?”

Back at the table, I kissed the top of Walton’s head and took Dot’s offered hand. In case it’s not apparent, I adored those two passionate eccentrics.

“Postcards, please,” Walton asked.

“Daily,” I lied.

Dot chuckled as I opened the door.

***

Looking back into their yard of deep beautiful snow, there were Walton’s footprints leading from her Airstream to Dot’s. Raising my hands before my eyes and touching my thumbs and pointer fingers, I formed a viewfinder, framing the image. I admired the symmetry of the composition, two homes linked by a willingness to remember what was significant: love. I was hopeful that the next time I visited, the footprints would still be crossing back and forth from his home to hers.

Lowering the viewfinder, I remembered the letter in my coat pocket and took it out, looking across the small clearing. Icy snow was falling and a wind was up.

"Are those flurries? Is that sleet? What is sleet?" I asked, turning for my Willy. No idea. All this snow world living was still novel and growing tedious.

Rather than open the envelope in the wind and sleet or whatever it was, I carried it from the side yard of Gustin's Packard Restorations. Climbing inside the Willy, I started the engine and sat, basking in the hot blowing air.

"Read it when I get home," I told the dashboard. "Got something else to think on."

That morning's Mexican newspapers had called him Jappy the Killer. A twelve-year-old boy with lots of blood on his hands.

Was it him? Was that possible?

Chapter Three

The Lake Cottage

I could have headed back to the dealership for the rest of the day, but I didn't. Driving along Whitmore Lake Road, heading north, the world was white. And brutally cold.

The only other vehicle I saw was a brave and determined, tall brown UPS truck, creeping along like I was. The road between the drifts was packed snow over ice over crumbled, worn pavement.

"Thank you, Chrysler." They were the maker of Jeeps. Squinting through the windshield, the wipers were working their magic and manic best.

Three miles from my new hometown of Dent, I approached the bridge with its sign.

BRIDGE ICES BEFORE ROAD

Crossing it, the snow winds tried to sway the Willy.

"Thank you, Chrysler," I repeated, this time for the big strong tires under the heavy Jeep.

Along both sides of the road were strands of white dipped trees and snowfields.

A mile later, I entered a downhill run through a valley. After descending a third of the way, I downshifted and touched the brakes. The Willy didn't seem to understand what I was doing. At the bottom of the hill was an intersection.

The biggest tires and brakes can't beat black ice. I glided past the stop sign and through the intersection, the rear end of the Willy swinging out to the left, my eyes wide for any oncoming traffic from either side.

My hands clenching the steering wheel, I brought the slide under control as I started up the other side.

Although I couldn't see it, the last run to Dent was on a dirt road of frozen puddles and tire ruts. All I could see was the endless white snow being swept by the wipers, the headlights boring two tunnels through the falling, swirling storm.

Entering the small town of Dent, its main street looked abandoned. Except for the *Pawn & Gold – We Buy!* the shops opposite the lake were dark and dead, no doorways shoveled, no business until summer. On the last corner was the Lake Dent Tavern. Of course, *it* was open, with a half dozen pickups in the driveway. Up above, the town's single traffic light swung like a corpse in the snow-filled gusts, casting a useless, yellow cautionary glow. I used the blinkers, like anyone was around to see them, and steered onto the twisting road along the frozen lake. The shore was lined with cottages like mine, nearly all darkened; sensible owners don't return until summer.

To my left was Lake Dent, a solid block of ice. As always, I visualized the fish. Not knowing what else they could do, I *saw* the fish frozen, mid-bubble until spring. Shaking that image off, I parked in my driveway and climbed out, relieved to be off the roads.

The cruel stairs down to the simple front door were on the side of the cottage. Cruel because of the iced winds blowing across that frozen lake and striking me right in the face. Since I left for the dealership that morning, the steep wood stairs had a foot and a half of snow, looking innocent like a row of cakes with frosting. I knew better. Under that snow was ice that would love to help me down after a single step. There was this bucket of some salt-like stuff I kept forgetting to sprinkle on them.

Holding the handrail, I minced my steps down to the porch like a tottering old fool.

On a drift alongside my front door was a FedEx parcel that I carried inside. Seeing that the return address was Pauline's attorneys, I set it on the entrance table. I was headed for the kitchen, where I kept my Jappy the Killer files, clippings, and notes.

I crossed the small main room of my neat and tidy home—neat and tidy was my way. On the table before the couch was my latest effort at designing a new movie camera viewfinder, an orderly rows of parts and tools. The kitchen housed my second obsession; the table covered with all the documents Rhonda had sent me.

Taking off my coat, I removed the letter from its pocket and held it in both hands—there was no return address. The envelope looked like it had had a rough journey from Jalisco, Mexico, identified by the postage. I looked at the address on the envelope. Between my name and the dealership's street address was a c/o. It read "Regarding Jappy el Niño Asesino."

With a steak knife at the sink, I slit it open and sat down at the table. The letter was folded twice. Opening it, I read.

Senor Danser,

We are aware of your inquiries into the identification of the niño so often referred to as Jappy el Niño Asesino. We are writing to inform you that this coldhearted street urchin has been captured and imprisoned as deserved. He awaits trial on several serious charges, many of them homicides for hire. Our evidence is watertight and we are confident that he will never again see the light of day.

While we are perplexed by your interest in this case, we want to ensure you that all has been done to remove him from the streets forever. As I am sure you can understand, many of the details of our investigation cannot be shared. We can tell you that this Jappy, as he is so called, is a native Mexican from the state of Tlaxcala, where he has been a criminal since the age of seven. His records are a long, unfortunate story of ever worse offenses.

Having shared all that we can with you, we are confident that your inquires can end.

Sinceramente,
Sargent Luiz Bonfá
Policía estatal de Jalisco – División de Warrants

Cc: A copy of this letter has gone to your investigator at the Blue Wave Movie Company.

Taking out my cellphone, I laid it on the table beside the letter and tapped Rhonda's number. She picked up on the third ring, and I said, "Hey ya."

"Hey, ya, I made some calls as soon as my copy arrived. Pie? It's a joke. And not the ha-ha kind. This Sargent Luiz Bonfá doesn't exist in that miserable excuse of a police department."

Rhonda had dropped the Dixie-chick accent for her focused and amped-up business voice. I appreciated the change.

"Thank you for Res'ing that," I said, *Res* being our nickname for research.

"Welcome. It's what I do best."

"Can we find out who sent it?" I asked.

"Of course. I've got the time and you've got the money. Barely."

"The letter looks official. Whoever took some time…" I said.

"They clearly think we're a couple of dipsticks," Rhonda said.

"I suggest you let me send a reply. I'll tell this ass hat that we are ending the inquiries and thank him and all that. You good with that?"

"Yes, good idea. Thank you."

"*In other news*," Rhonda continued, mocking a newscaster's voice, "heard back from that Carson Staines. Wants a laughable amount to talk to me. I agreed, only to stall him while I take another route. Have a friend down in IT who's going to help me with that. You can afford her. Barely."

"Barely," I said. "Illegal?" I asked.

"Of course. Let's get straight to the heart of all this. After I dust our trail with that fake cop, I'll go downstairs and kick off the search."

"You are the best."

"Dontcha know it." She eased back into southern twang. "Gotta run. The boss wants me to do some studio work of all things."

"Call me anytime."

"Soon as sumthing shakes loose."

We ended the call. My thoughts turned to Pauline. Damn, I wanted to talk this puzzle over with her. She had a way of sorting through a pile of scattered pieces to place the important ones, pointing me in the best direction.

I looked up and out through the rear cottage window. I wanted to call. Instead, I stalled.

Just past the snow-white lawn was my damaged, leaning dock, extending out over the ice that had gripped and twisted the planks. I hadn't known to dismantle the dock sections and store them in the fall. I was reminded daily by this view.

Rhonda had located the cottage for me when I was opening the dealership. She told me some Danser clan in Florida owned it. I had never met them.

"Since you've got the same last name, you get a key," she explained.

My dad, BB, had been here when he was about the same age as the boy in Mexico. BB visited the cottage with his father and was present when his father's girlfriend turned a shotgun on her lover. BB once told me that his father was buried here where he dropped, somewhere back of the cottage.

Speaking of cheery family events, Christmas was just around the corner. My plans? Hazy. The day before, I had kicked around the idea of spending the holiday aboard the boat Pauline gave me, *The Viewfinder*. It was in a slip at the Detroit Yacht Club, on the private island adjacent to Belle Isle. The boat was delivered three years earlier after being navigated through the locks and canals linking the Great Lakes to the Atlantic. It would be familiar but also haunted. I need to think more about that.

I did know the cottage wasn't going to work. The place was as sad as a single man's last lonely residence. Ideal for a car salesman in the frozen dead of winter with a fridge full of Swanson dinners in foil. Which it was. Thank the stars, I no longer guzzled alcohol. There would then be a grocery box of bottles, and what next? Buy a television?

With a shake of my head, I picked up my copy of the last known photograph of Jappy the Killer. His back was turned, facing the open side of a tent a dozen feet in from of him. There again was that baseball cap with its half of a golden letter P in his young hand.

My plans for the rest of the day? Definitely not opening the FedEx parcel with the divorce documents.

I left the table and went upstairs to my bedroom, where I kept a lockbox holding my passport. Pocketing it, I packed a suitcase.

"I'll head out in the morning," I told my little room: bed, table, lamp. That's all.

"First stop will be the dealership. Lease myself the Willy."

What else could I do with this mystery?

Drive to Kansas, of course.

Chapter Four

First Light

The first light of dawn arrived hidden by dark gray clouds. My bedroom windowsill held nearly a foot of frozen snow pressed against the glass. I showered and dressed and found my ancient briefcase in the utility room. After packing up the Jappy files in it, I took my packed suitcase in my other hand and opened the front door. Fresh snow had frozen overnight. There on the table just inside was the FedEx parcel of divorce documents. Bringing them along felt like I was tainting my road trip, but I couldn't avoid the hard choice forever. That decided, I put them inside the briefcase, stepped out, and locked up my shoebox on the lake. I was tempted to form a viewfinder with my thumbs and forefingers for a parting image, but it was so damned cold.

After snow kicking my way up the stairs to the driveway, the Willy looked like a block of ice with a layer of snow on top.

Scraping the windows clear, I sat inside that block, shaking and trembling until the heater was blowing hot and strong. The tires crunched and cracked a path back out onto the lake road, and I headed out, not looking back.

The roads were a hazard. While the drifts and unplowed way looked soft and white, a thick deep glaze of ice had been laid down through the night. Driving ridiculously far under the speed limit, the twisting road traced the contour of the lake. I left the small town of Dent and made my way south to the dealership.

Parking out front and leaving the Willy running, I went inside to my office. Sam Says was at his desk, bug eyes to his large monitor, his hands massaging his mouse and keyboard. After pulling the title docs for the Willy, I sat down long enough to take my checkbook out and write the first lease payment. Signing it, I walked over to Sam's office and knocked on the glass doorframe.

"I'm going to be gone for a while; think you can handle the crowd of customers?"

I got the expected smirk.

His eyes were glued to whatever was on the screen. I wasn't the least bit curious.

"Rest of the day?" he asked

"Rest of a few days. Maybe longer."

"Today? Don't you watch the news? We're having an ice storm."

I didn't know what an ice storm was, but it didn't sound like fun.

"I'll be on the highways. They should be plowed."

Sam Says looked up at that.

"*Should* be, yes. I'd wait until the storm blows through. At least stop at a market and get an emergency stash of snacks."

I saw myself trying to live in the snow-trapped Willy on the side of some forgotten stretch of highway. Running the engine until the last drop of gasoline was spent. Peeing out the door. My own private Donner party. Ending that tragic movie in my head, I set the transfer doc and check on the edge of his desk.

"I have my cellphone."

It sounded as lame as it was.

His desk phone rang, surprising both of us. We looked at the little blinking light.

"That can't be good," Sam said. "Bet it's Jeep-Chrysler again."

The phone rang a second time, a third, a fourth.

"Could be a customer," I offered.

Laughing, Sam picked up the receiver and I left the dealership.

***

Two miles up Whitmore Lake Road, I pulled into the area's only gas station. After topping off the tank, I went inside the Quickee Mart for two bottles of Fanta grape soda and a family pack of beef jerky. Tempted to buy a plastic bucket to pee in, I passed, ever hopeful. At the front of the store, I spun the map display until I found one that covered the Midwest.

The salesclerk was in an early morning stupor, offering me a thousand-miles-away gaze and a smile that pained her.

"Shouldn't be out in all that," she warned me with a nod to the plate glass windows.

"Thank you," was all I could find to say. I certainly didn't have a sensible argument for being *out in all that.*

Opening the map on the passenger seat, I traced the line of highways south and under the belly of Lake Michigan and then west into Illinois. It looked to me like I could be in Missouri by the middle of the day. Get a hotel, a meal, some sleep, and be in Kanas by the middle of the next day.

I liked the idea that I was heading in a slight southern direction, away from the frigid storms in the north. By then, I would surely have new information from Rhonda. Who knows, maybe she could weasel a photograph of Jappy the Killer that included his mysterious face?

Motoring slow and safe, I drove along unplowed roads to the highway entrance. Accelerating cautiously up the entrance ramp, the world had changed for the worse. No longer white, I was in the land of gray fog and the harsh clicking of ice striking the roof and windshield. I had the slow lane all to myself, all wise souls except long-haul truck drivers having the sense to stay home safe and warm. Thirty miles an hour felt sketchy, so slowed to twenty-five, hoping not to get rear-ended by some brave or foolish trucker.

I relaxed in the seat as best I could, but my hands were clenched white on the steering wheel. Before me was a long day of this. Slow mile after mile would turn into the tens and then the hundreds. I only needed to keep the Willy on the pavement that I couldn't see, the tires humming on the scraped dirty snow and ice. If I were a radio person, which I am not, I would have the stereo on a soothing channel of classical music working on my mind like a calming movie soundtrack. Instead, I stared forward to keep the Willy aimed true, trying not to look into the rearview mirrors too much. I focused on where I was going rather than worrying about racing headlights about to smash me off the road and into a snowbank.

Passing under the first bridge along that stretch of Highway 23, the windshield exploded.

A spray of glass and wind blasted me in the face. The back of my head slammed the headrest. I was blinded. Stunned and yelling, ice and shards dashed my face and hands as the interior became a swirling, freezing cyclone.

My foot went hard on the brakes, only making things worse. The Willy slurred sideways.

Hard snow was thrown up over the hood and in on me. Twisting the wheel to the left, I tried to counter the slide. The big tires turned and the ice laughed at that. The tail of the Willy slung around. I saw roadside trees closing. Metal crunched and the right side of the Jeep climbed skyward. Impact with the guardrail fired off the airbag, bashing me in the face and chest.

With my hands and arms knocked away, the Willy careened of the metal. Steering itself, parts flying, the Jeep chose its path. Pirouetting, it took me back across the highway to the concrete divider. The second impact was brutal, stopping everything with a loud rending and scattering of parts.

The motor was still running, sounding mortally wounded but alive, steam and smoke struggling upward against the falling ice and snow.

Batting down the airbag, I brushed glass from my face, the ice rain coming in through the missing windshield. The cold was numbing, or maybe it was shock. I sat wide-eyed, staring at the destroyed right side of the Jeep, the fender and hood tilted, the metal bent, forming creases that were filling fast from above.

A new fear screamed like an alarm in my head. What was coming up through the fog from behind? I spun around on the seat.

Headlights were approaching, up high, taller than those of a car. They were turning to avoid me, plowing snow and ice upward as it crashed into the drift next to my lane. The big rig's horn was blaring one long howl. I cowered against my door; eyes squeezed tight for the impact.

A wave of ice wind rocked my destroyed heavy vehicle. The long-haul truck roared past, its large wheels inches from the Willy, horn still blasting.

A first, I was tempted to climb out and run somewhere, anywhere, for safety. But instead, I stayed inside the solid husk of the Willy, turning on the emergency flashers, my hand searching the passenger seat for my phone while staring back up the road behind the accident.

I dialed 9-1-1 and reported the accident, estimating my location.

"Already have it," I was told. "A trucker called it in."

Staring back up the road for whatever might smash into the Willy, I watched a slowing car plow through the drift between the lanes, sending up a heavy spray of gray and white. Oncoming traffic slowed, but it would only take one distracted driver to start a ricochet of vehicles smashing into others.

Another big rig came to a complete stop twenty yards back, its tires straddling the middle of the two lanes. The driver switched on his emergency flashers and climbed out with a canvas bag of road flares. Before I climbed out to help him, I placed a second call.

Ryan Dot would come to my rescue, but I opted for Sam Says, who was surely not as busy.

"How're they hanging?" Sam answered. I hoped he answered that way because he recognized my number.

"Call me a tow truck, please."

"So soon?"

"So soon. I'm just aways down South 23."

"I'll call Brighton's."

"Thank you," I hung up and climbed out.

Crossing to the trucker in the icy wind, my head was down, eyes forward. He handed me three flares without a word, pointing to the left rear of his extended trailer. I lit one flare after another, the fiery red flame glaring where I set each back along the road.

The state police arrived a few minutes later. One cruiser and then a second. They took quick and effective control of the situation, one of the officers coordinating with the trucker, the other taking my arm gently and placing me inside the back seat of his vehicle.

The officer squatted before the open door. He looked me over before concentrating on my eyes, his expression distant but also concerned.

"Sir, are you okay? We can call EMS or get you off the road."

"I'm fine, thank you. Let's get out of the way."

"Good as done." He talked to his partner via his shoulder mic and climbed in behind the wheel, kindly cranking up the heater.

"Sir, what happened?" He steered slowly forward, not turning to me.

"Not sure, but it must have been ice falling from the bridge."

"Uh, huh. You saw it fall?"

"No, just the explosion."

"Explosion?"

"Yes, the windshield exploded."

"We don't get a lot of that happening, but today's not the norm." He sounded puzzled. "Sometimes a chuck will hit the glass and crack it. Strange."

I had nothing to say to that.

"Can you take meet me over to Brighton's?" I asked him. "A friend called for their tow truck." Brighton Wreckers and Auto Repair was the only repair shop within twenty-five miles of the dealership.

"Of course, sit back and relax. I'll check out your ID and registration when we get there."

We motored slowly along Highway 23 to the first off-ramp. While navigating the snow roads, he chatted with his dispatcher. I watched the white fields and occasional farmhouses pass by. By my calculation, I had made precisely seventeen miles on my great big road trip.

***

The Willy arrived on the back of Brighton's long tow truck, looking far from brand new. The right front side and the rear were demolished. I watched it being unloaded from inside the wrecker's small and cluttered front office.

Across the counter of photographs of other wrecks pressed under a sheet of glass was a woman in her fifties. She had a broad face of coarse skin under a great deal of makeup: vibrant red lipstick and hair in a nest of red tangles. Her expression was tired or bored. "Bridgette" was embossed on her shirt pocket. Under her name was "Owner," and she had taken to calling me "Hun," which was fine.

I took a chair with the offered clipboard of papers and a pen. I don't know why they needed to know, but the form asked, "Cause of Accident?"

I wrote "icicle."

Looking at that, I paused before adding a question mark.

I retrieved my suitcase and briefcase of Jappy files from the destroyed Willys by the time Sam Says rolled in.

"Were you drinking? he asked, checking out my eyes.

That was both offensive and a risk I ran daily, which he knew.

"Not even close. Got hit by falling ice." I walked to his car, a twenty-year-old Buick Park Avenue, pockmarked with rust from road salt.

"Where to? Home?" He steered us through the wrecking and repair yard and out to the gate.

"The dealership," I said, determined to make a bit more than seventeen miles on my trip in search of more pieces of the puzzle about that boy in Mexico.

"You got creamed by falling ice?" he asked, turning north.

"Yes, you know, an icicle."

"That took out the *entire* windshield? Never saw that before. Could it have been a gunshot? You know, both barrels blasting away?"

"Sam? Just drive. Please." That was not only a frightening thought but also ridiculous. Only from the mind of Sam Says, he of video games on his work computer.

***

Back inside the dealership, I went to my desk and wrote out a second check. Since all four Willys out on the lot were identical, I chose the one closest to the street.

We said our goodbyes, Sam thankfully only asking once, "You sure you have to go today? It's only getting uglier out."

That was true. The angry dark gray clouds were maybe a hundred feet over the dealership, unloading a hostile mix of fog, snow, and ice.

"Yes, thank you. I'll be taking it even slower."

He still hadn't asked where I was going, and I was grateful. Telling him my plan would have certainly amused him.

I went out the door, entering the cold, trudging through crunching drifts. Taking my suitcase and briefcase from his car, I put them in the backseat of my second Willy.

"Miles to go." I steered out onto the street, aiming the tires into the furrows from a prior vehicle. Carefully unlatching the briefcase and opening it on the passenger seat, there were the divorce documents ready for signature. I lifted them out and set them behind the briefcase lid—out of sight and out of mind. Mostly.

On top of the files was the gas station map and a packet of beef jerky. The two bottles of Fanta had disappeared somewhere along the way. No way would I attempt to open the map, but it was comforting to have it there beside me. I knew enough of this part of Michigan to take Highway 23 south to east-west Highway 94, which I believed would get me across the state and into the next.

Watching the road with alert, cautious eyes, I mentally formed a viewfinder, this one circular like that of a Panavision studio camera. As always throughout my life, the viewfinders, real or imagined, brought the important details into focus. Be it composing images or, like that day, the questions and puzzle pieces.

A small airplane crashed in the trees, falling to the jungle floor. A boy somehow survived that, crawling from the wreckage. He started climbing through the dense vegetation, making his way to civilization. Blood red headlines superimposed, screaming "Jappy Strikes Again?" Then, after a slow dissolve, there was the photograph taken by some reporter tracking the young killer. The imaged centered on the screen, and there was the boy with his back turned. His lovely, long black hair. That baseball cap.

The film paused. Many pieces were missing. Rhonda and I had much more to *res* to do. That said, I was on the road, headed for new information that would be painful, but had to be asked for. I accepted that but worried about opening fresh wounds in Kansas. A rise of hard snow bucked the steering, and I corrected without being distracted. The viewfinder held true, the facts and questions not shaken. There it was, written in dramatic full-screen movie text.

IS IT POSSIBLE? IS THE BOY MY GRANDSON?

Chapter Five

Decatur

Heading out again across unsaddled America, I left Michigan and drove down across the belly of Illinois. Having escaped the ice storm, I traveled the highways of white snow. I found it best to trail big rigs, no matter the constant spray of wet road grime that the wipers did a great job of cleaning. Three hours along, I was in a road-trip stupor, slow mile after mile under cloudy skies releasing large flakes of snow, the highway plowed but quickly filling again.

I had a travel partner of sorts, a gray Jaguar on the same route. The Jag stood out in the Midwest like a foreign object, which it was. We played hopscotch through the hours and miles. When the Jag first passed me, I saw it was badly in need of a wash, its flanks filthy, its dirty windshield two half-moons from the wipers, the glass otherwise a tired brown-gray. A woman was at the wheel. I only saw her profile; she never looked across.

Somewhere along the way, I stopped to fill the tank and buy a bottle of grape soda. Back out in the winter wonderland, I ate beef jerky from the briefcase, wondering how far I would make it that first day.

It turns out, I made a slow but steady three hundred eighty-five miles to the highway town of Decatur, Illinois. With nightfall closing, I searched the off-ramp marquees for hotel signs, not feeling brave enough to continue driving the winter roads in darkness.

The Decatur Inn was a two-story, dirt brown row hotel. Forty-five dollars a night. The sign out front offered:

WEEKLY RATES, FRIDGE & MICRO, WIFI

I climbed from the warm, modern cocoon of the Willy and out into blowing winds of dime-sized snowflakes. The skin of my face stunned by the cold, I hurried across the parking lot to the motel office. I wanted to run but didn't want to slip and break my neck.

A dog was curled up in the alcove outside the door, searching for cover from the winds. It could have been mistaken for a filthy abandoned mop head. I opened the door and propped it with my rear, the winds shoving at it.

"Hello, can I let him in?" I gestured to the dog.

"No."

"He's shivering."

"Close that door; you're letting the cold in."

I saw why he didn't want the sad trembling small dog inside: competition. The motel manager already had two dogs of his own. I stepped inside and the door closed at my heels.

"How many nights?" the man behind the desk asked. He was short and immensely wide. I pitied the chair supporting him.

"One," I said, looking at his two pets. When I was a kid, we called them wienie dogs. Long, brown and black with narrow snouts. They were seated side by side on a low table under the side window that faced the road. The dogs were staring at me with steady black glass eyes.

Taxidermy - for that perfect pet. Coming soon, services for spouses.

Shaking that thought off, I paid for the room, got a key on

a fob, and left. Crossing to the Willy, I grabbed my suitcase and briefcase and the pack of beef jerky. Kneeling in front of the car door, I poured the dark dried meat on the concrete in front of the shaking dog. It was the size of a loaf of bread with a head. The dog ate slowly, like doing so was pointless. Shivering myself, I nonetheless remained on my haunches, watching him finish his meal. When he looked up, I saw that he was missing his right eye.

"C'mon," I said, standing.

The good eye stared up at me. The dog wasn't in the mood for tail wagging.

"You can have the second bed," I told him. "Do you snore?" I asked.

He climbed to his little legs. I walked a few feet away and turned. He was eyeing me, looking uncertain.

"Come along, Fido," I encouraged, no idea where "Fido" came from but probably a movie. He took a tentative step forward.

I crossed the lot and unlocked my room. Holding the door open and looking at him, the warmth of the room must have made the deal. He entered, looking side to side but not stopping until he found the heater vent under the sink in the rear of the room. He had been white once upon a time but was then a tangle of gray and brown fur. While he curled up, I went back out to the Willy. I drove over to a diner a half-mile away and bought enough hamburgers for two.

After we had dined in silence, I kicked off my shoes and lay down on the bed with my cellphone.

"What's your name?" I asked the dog as I dialed Rhonda's number. His head rose, but he didn't reply. As the phone rang, I thought, *A pet? Me? I'll get a dog when I'm ninety, and all my friends and loves are dead. Someone to talk to and argue with.*

"Hey ya," Rhonda answered, "think I shook the right tree down there."

"Hey ya. Which tree?"

"Federales. A Lieutenant De Los Santos with decent English

and limited access to the airport shooting files. We talked for twenty minutes. I said limited because the investigation team is cutting back. He's been reassigned. So ya know, you wired him five hundred dollars. A donation to his favorite charity. Wanna guess which one?"

"His retirement fund?"

"Yep. The remaining officers on the team have no fresh leads. They're reviewing past interviews, going back through the files; in other words, spinning. They're looking at a suspicious murder north of Puerto Mita at some remote hotel where witnesses will be questioned about a boy possibly being involved. All De Los Santos knows is that it's been reported that the boy is not a local."

"Do they have any photographs of him?"

"Not a one but what's been in the newspapers."

"But maybe witnesses who saw his face?"

"Maybe, yes. He promised to call me after the hotel interviews. For another donation, of course."

"Anything on that Carson Staines?"

"Another greedy mother-humper. He's willing to forward *some* of his notes. Piecemeal. Different prices based on content. I have a call with him in a few minutes. Speaking of money, *your* money, Pie, you leased two jeeps in one day? You're no longer rich. You could be if you signed the you-know-what docs."

"I'm thinking on that," I lied. "Does the reporter have any photographs of the boy's face he's willing to sell?"

"That's on my list of questions. The first time I asked, he got all cute and elusive. I wouldn't be surprised if he wants to sell those piecemeal as well. Know what I think?"

"Tell me."

"The boy somehow escaped and is running. Let me talk with this ball sack writer, see what he says. I'll call you back. Probably take a half-hour."

"Rhonda?"

"Yep?"

"Thank you."

No witty retort. Twenty seconds of silence. Then her voice, soft, without edge or wit.

"Thank you, Pie. For letting me help. I want to find him as well."

Setting the phone aside on the bed, I built a viewfinder with my fingers and thumbs. Images connected like a dot to dot. There were missing snapshots, but enough there for a short vignette.

The crashed Cessna. A boy climbing from the jungle. Surviving somehow in the alleys and back streets of a foreign country. A question mark appeared on the center screen. Then the words:

HOW DOES A FARM BOY BECOME A KILLER?

The viewfinder panned over the blood-red Mexican headlines, featuring "Jappy el Niño Asesino." I blinked, and the viewfinder gave me the photo of the back of the long-haired boy: he and his baseball cap. I adjusted the zoom to the gold, half-letter P. Another question typed across the screen.

WHERE IS HE?

I added stock footage of an airport and hotel witnesses being questioned. The ending was also the final question. Was it him?

I climbed off the bed and ran a shower.

Using soap and a washrag, I rubbed the three hundred eighty-five miles from my face and thoughts. Rinsing off, I stood under the stream with pieces of the Jappy puzzle still trying to fit together.

The shower curtain stirred. I parted it, and there was the dog, looking like roadkill. I held out my hands. He seemed receptive, so I gingerly lifted him over the tub side and down between my feet. After he had soaked in the clean, warm water, I poured shampoo along his spine and gently lathered him up. Dirt and grime poured from his fur. Gray and brown soapy water swirled the drain.

Kneeling and dripping wet, I toweled him off first. After he shook a few times, he showed the first sign of life: the slightest of a tail wag while nosing the door open and leaving the bathroom.

I dried off, hand combed my hair in the mirror, and turned off the light. The dog was lying sphinxlike in front of his heater vent. I climbed into bed to wait for Rhonda's call.

The cellphone purred and I sat up.

"Hello, Pierce," Rhonda said, voice flat and low.

"Where's my hey ya?"

"Can't find it. Took another call while waiting for the journal-ist to answer."

"And?"

"A cowboy named Rex. Said he's a U.S. Marshal working both sides of the border. He was calling from Brownsville, Texas, just across the border with Mexico. He refused to give me his last name."

"And?"

"Asked why a movie studio was sniffing around in Puerto Mita. He's clearly got an inside with the Mexican authorities."

"A U.S. Marshal?"

"Since I don't know him from dick, I told him we were doing a little research for a possible film about the Mexican kids who are killing for the cartels. I asked for his badge number. He chuckled. No, really, a *chuckle*. All gravelly. That's not all; this big tough Texan has a lisp."

"Like what? A gay cowboy?"

"Might be. Or has a mouth injury. Called me honey like five times. Also told me the Mexicans want nothing to do with a movie about punks like Jappy, 'just another dead-eyed kid with a pistol.'"

"Does this mean the U.S. Marshals are looking for the boy?"

"If he's legit. I did a search on his number. He did call from Brownsville, but from a personal phone, not a government one. Get this, Pie. He also said, '*Missy*, you don't stop. You're going to lose your snout in a claw trap.' Pie, that sounded like a threat to me. I told him so. He laughed and told me, 'Honey, don't get your tits in the ringer.' Before I had a chance to climb through the telephone line and rip the grin off that smug cowboy's face, he hung up with a parting shot. 'Jappy's got a big red target on his back, so piss off Miss Hollywood, or you will too.'"

"Give me his number. Better yet, see if you can find out who his boss is and give me that one."

"Will do. While he was talking, I received an email from Carson Staines. No need for a call, he says. Attached was a list of prices for his notes, in three groups."

"Any photographs?"

"None offered. He's my next call. By the way, do you remember how to get to the farm?" Rhonda's spirits had lightened with the change of topic.

"I know it's somewhat near Hutchinson."

"Jeez. You in a hotel? Gimme your hotel fax number. I'll send you directions."

I found the fax number on the cardboard triangle on the nightstand and read it to her.

"I'll send them tonight," Rhonda said. "Pie? I think the boy is alive and might have escaped."

"I'm thinking so, too."

"A lot of people really don't want you finding him."

"Yes. All the more reason to…" I trailed off. While puzzled, I was also determined.

"I agree." Rhonda ended my thought and the call. "Let's find him."

Chapter Six

Bill

At sunrise, I walked over to the motel office, turned in my key, and asked for my faxes. The dog followed me to the office and out to the Willy, where I loaded the suitcase in the back seat. The two of us stood in the parking lot for our goodbyes. I stalled, asking the dog, "Wanna go on a road trip?" I got the slightest of a tail wag. After opening the passenger door, he jumped in.

Leaving Decatur, we headed out across Illinois on Highway 70. I placed the directions from Rhonda inside my open briefcase on the passenger seat, the dog laying on the floorboard. An hour along, we got ourselves a drive-through breakfast and I filled the tank. After that, it was miles of silence, driving southwest, the roads freshly plowed, drifts along both sides, the sky a low and oppressive gray.

Adding to the somber mood was the worry about where I was headed. Was I delivering hope? Or heartache and newly opened wounds? It was all good and fine for me to be chasing after the ghost of that boy, but I was now about seven hours from including his parents in my windmill pursuit.

I called my best friend, Ryan Dot.

"Hey there," I greeted him. "How are things?"

"I'm calling today good and amusing. What are you up to?"

"Headed to Mexico," I paused and added, "making a side trip to Kansas," knowing he would know what that meant.

"Oh," he said slowly.

"Oh?"

"If you think that's best, I'm with you."

"Thank you. I think it's best if they know what I'm doing."

"Yes…"

"But if I'm wrong, I'm delivering hurt, and they've had so much."

"They certainly have. Give me a second…"

"Of course."

This was true of Dot. He was one of those rare types who did a bit of thinking before offering advice.

"Here's this," he said. "One: if there is a possibility it's him, you're doing good. Two: I agree that they should know what you're up to. Give them a chance to help, assuming they don't run your sorry, delusional ass of their property."

I could hear Dot's grin in the last.

Walton was yelling in the background.

"What's Walton up to?" I asked.

"She's outside on the porch, kicking and cursing our snowblower."

"She'll show it who's who."

"I've no doubt."

"Assuming I don't put the Willy in a ditch, I'll be at the farm later today."

"Good. I bet it'll be a delight to see them. Christmas in Kansas and all that. If it helps, you're bringing a gift of sorts. Hope."

What do I say to that? I felt renewed.

"Thank you again, Dot. Now get off the phone and go help our favorite Walton."

"On it. Call anytime."

We ended the call.

Placing the nose of the Willy in the draft of a long-haul eighteen-wheeler, I let it lead the way. It felt safer and slower, which was fine with me; I was no longer in a rush.

I saw the dirty gray Jaguar from the day before near Topeka, after crossing the border from Missouri into Kansas. That woman seriously needed to find a car wash, although the once clean, white Willy was also road splashed, with sides of brown and gray. The Jag passed me and took the next off-ramp. Possibly for a drive through a rinse and wash?

The miles rolled on. The dog had the right response to the dull, endless country. He was curled up on the passenger floorboard, sleeping under the heat vent. Rhonda's faxed directions had me turn from Highway 70 onto I135, heading south.

By the middle of the afternoon, I was driving bland, boring miles of farmlands. The fields stretched to the horizons, endless acres of green winter wheat on both sides of the two-lane with its ditches full of snow. Far off to the east, a storm was rolling across the plains. Boiling dark clouds, like bad omens, were chasing me.

I slowed up for the last fifteen miles. I had a story to tell and wanted to get it right. If I were brave enough to lift my hands from the wheel, I would have formed a viewfinder to help me compose all I knew and didn't know. Keeping the Willy aimed straight, I resorted to a mental viewfinder. In it, the puzzle pieces formed an incomplete story, but a story, nonetheless. It came to me that what was important was how I told the story, with love and kindness and, as Dot said, with hope.

Their long driveway was the first touch of the familiar, having visited twice before, most recently for the memorial service two years back. Listening to the tires crunching along the gravel, the barn drew closer, off to the left, its large doors open. Beyond was their farmhouse, windows warmed by amber light.

I parked beside Bill's old jeep with its big dirty tires, alongside Ali's flatbed truck. Light was spilling from the barn's interior between a thresher and a seed trailer behind a tractor. I climbed out, the dog following me, and looked for a sign of my son.

Dan the Baby appeared, peeking from the side of the large door to the right, eyes ignoring me, looking in wonderment at the dog at my side. The three-year-old boy with his long first name was beaming with curiosity.

"Hello, Dan, you're looking fine. Remember me?"

"Yes." He didn't look up at me. Instead, he walked from the big door of the three-story barn to the dog.

"What's its name?" Dan the Baby asked.

"Roadkill," I decided. "We just met."

Dan the Baby was delighted. Roadkill raised his leg on the child's little work boot and relieved himself.

Dan the Baby laughed, his eyes bright with surprise and amusement. He lowered and gave Roadkill a head-to-tail petting.

"Know where your dad is?" I lowered beside my adorable, happy grandson.

"In the barn," he said absently, stroking the dog back and forth.

I looked across the driveway.

Bill was at the left side workbench just inside the barn, cleaning his hands with balm and a rag. He was studying me without a word, just a smile.

"Dad? This is great." He tossed the rag on the workbench and started across. He was beaming. So was I.

Stepping away from Dan the Baby and Roadkill, I walked to my son and took him in my arms, feeling him pull me close, his strong hand slapping my back.

"Any special occasion?" He leaned away, smiling, hands on my shoulders, looking into my eyes.

I thought on that a moment like Dot had taught me to do.

"I've got a story to tell," was the best I could say, looking at my son's handsome face; his eyes smart and tinged with a sadness that he lived with every day.

"Can't wait, let me guess," he said. "You've decided to chuck the dealership and buy a farm?"

We both laughed.

"Even I'm not that deranged," I said. I admired the world that Bill and Ali had built for themselves, but there'd be no farm life for me.

"Got yourself a pet."

"Yes, couldn't find a reasonable taxidermist."

"Meaning?"

"It's a joke."

"Perfectly random. Good. Let's go over to the house."

I readily agreed; the afternoon was cold and only getting colder.

"Come along," he called to his three-year-old son.

"Can he come?" Dan the Baby called back, arms around Roadkill.

"Up to Grandpa."

"*Grandpa*?" I frowned before grinning. "That will never work for me."

"...Up to this strange ex-cameraman."

"Better."

The three of us walked over to the house, Dan the Baby struggling with Roadkill in his arms. The dog looked to be loving those little arms embracing him.

We entered their home through the back door into the winter porch where the family's coats and boots lined both walls. Kicking off our shoes and hanging our coats, I followed Bill and his youngest son into the kitchen, which was warm and bright. The warmth included the delicious scent of meat and onions and carrot pies in the oven. The house was also filled with music, discordant 1950s jazz—Ali's preference, which my son turned down as we entered the family room.

"Something to eat or drink?" Bill asked.

We smiled. Drink was something we both had a history

with—specifically, alcohol. Bill and I lived with and shared the same fear: the seduction of deadly Miss Icy Cocktails.

"Nothing, thank you," I replied, watching Dan the Baby place Roadkill on the couch and climb up beside him. Bill joined them, and I walked to the big window facing their backyard. Beyond were what looked like a million miles of short green winter wheat.

"Dad? The story?"

How had my son and his wife memorialized their other lost son? One of their ways was floating in their backyard—the boy's hand-built pirate boat in the steaming, heated swimming pool.

"Dad?"

Turning from the view, I saw the boy's face in a framed photograph on the back wall with other family portraits.

"Where's Ali?" I stalled, searching for the right words, the best way to begin.

"With her cameras," Bill said.

"It's about…" I stopped short of using their son's name. It had been a long time since I'd said it.

"Rhonda and I have been looking into what happened two years ago," was an easier way into the telling.

I took the recliner beside Bill on the couch.

"I'm headed to Mexico," I continued. "There is a possibility, and just that…"

"Yes?"

"I don't want to upset you and Ali. Don't ever want to hurt either of you..."

"Dad? Stop circling whatever it is."

I rested my hand on his knee.

"There are stories about a boy in the papers down there. In the Puerto Mita area. No one knows where he's from, but some believe he's American. There are some photographs, but they're incomplete. We have confirmed that he's now twelve years old. Some say he wandered in from the jungles."

"Dad. Stop. I don't know what lark you're on, but you know as well as I do that we received the coroner's report, the photos of the crash. Ali and I met with the authorities down there many times. You know that. They did a thorough investigation."

"Yes, I know."

Bill stood, my hand falling from his knee. Looking out the window, he went on. "Some days, it's all I can do not to start cracking open bottles of Tanqueray."

"Same. Faintly."

"Yes, thank the stars, it's faint these days. We didn't even have his body to bring home. They explained, again and again, that's what happens when someone dies in the jungle."

"Yes, I know. And that's certainly what happened. What Rhonda and I are—"

"All they found of my son were bits of… bloody clothing," Bill stopped, his hand pressing the window. "Now you come to us with another one of your mysterious *what if's*."

There was nothing to counter that. He was right.

"We haven't moved on. Not possible. But we also accept. There's no other way to stay upright."

I got to my feet and crossed and stood beside him, not touching him, though I wanted to. Before us, the sun was lowering, its light spraying through openings in the gray clouds.

"Accepting is the right thing to do," I said softly. "It is brave and best."

"Seems like someone we both know well hasn't got there yet."

That stung, as it should.

"Know what?" Bill turned from the window and joined his youngest son on the couch, "You tell Ali. It's your story, not mine."

Chapter Seven

Ali

I left the house, rounding the swimming pool with the small pirate boat floating in the warm waters, almost hidden in the fog from the steam. Passing their ancient shade tree, there was the mud and gravel field road. With Bill having told me that Ali was "with her cameras," I knew where I would find her.

Walking a quarter mile along, I stepped from the road and entered the six-hundred-acre field back of the house. In the distance was the largest standing ladder I had ever seen, easily eighty feet tall. It was twice the size of the last one Ali had built.

Looking down to keep my shoes in the crop furrows, I didn't hurry; in fact, I lagged along. As with Bill, I approached the wonderful Ali with my odd sack of half-baked what ifs and scattered puzzle pieces.

Stopping halfway, I saw Ali standing beside a simple table where she kept her box of lenses, cameras, and film canisters. The frightening tall ladder stood at her back. She hadn't noticed me; her head was down, eyes focused on the table. Her movements looked somewhat stilted, not natural, but she was a fifty yards away.

Ali and her cameras and ladders; a constant during all the

years I had known her.

From our conversations, I had learned this had been an endeavor started a little while after the death of her first husband, a fellow grad school student on a visa from Kyoto, Japan.

The first husband had died right there on the farm. Trapped in the basement of the original home, the fire lit by his own hand. His madness, his decision, fueled by alcohol.

Ali once told me, "He was a fine father and a grenade. Taking a drink, he pulled his pin."

There's a wall in her and Bill's home office with a selection of her photographs. Different seasons, different heights. All the compositions were the same. Some in black and white. Most in color: their home and their fields.

The last time I was there with them was the day of their son's memorial. Ali had slipped away as soon as she politely could. The photograph of their farm taken from high above on that day included the cars and pickups of their caring neighbors.

During my last visit, Bill offered to lease Ali a safe cherry picker truck. He had also looked into how much a Liebherr mobile construction crane would cost.

"You're missing the point again," she replied, kissing him with smiling eyes.

I agreed with her.

"It's not just about the perspective; it's also about the climb," she told Bill.

***

I started walking the row again, the short wheat brushing my pants cuffs, taking my story to the boy's beautiful, creative, and resilient mother.

I studied her hand-built eighty-foot ladder. The winds crossing the fields were no longer a worry. The bottom rung was fifteen feet wide, with the legs set in concrete.

Her stiff movements explained themselves as I drew closer. Her broken left shoulder and elbow were in a cast. She was loading fresh film into her 1957 Hasselblad, one of the finest still cameras ever made, if a bit temperamental.

"Hello, Ali," I said softly, not to startle her.

"Know that voice." She smiled down at her fingers. "Hello, Pie. Come for Christmas?"

"Don't think so. Just passing through."

"Shame. Dan the Baby would love a grandpa holiday. Where are you headed?"

"Mexico."

She looked up at that.

"Why?" she asked. A breeze crossed the field, sweeping her auburn back from her lovely curious eyes.

"Rhonda and I have been looking into… the plane crash," I said quietly, gently as I could.

"I'll repeat myself. Why?" She set the camera down on her table.

It was the perfect question. Why was I dredging up their loss with my suspicions? I felt regret; I shouldn't have come, dragging my puzzle into their lives and laying it at their feet.

"I think there is a *possibility*—" I started.

"Love you, Pie, but what the fuck," she cut me off in a flash of anger.

I wanted to do nothing more than apologize, get in the Willy, and slink away.

"Right. Yes."

"We've already buried an empty casket. Some of his favorite books and drawings inside."

I stood there, like some insensitive ghoul.

"Let's head inside. I'm losing the light." Ali placed her cameras, lenses, and film canisters in a wood box. That done, she looked to me, most of the hurt and anger extinguished.

"Getting a fresh snowfall tonight." Her voice and eyes were

distant.

"Want me to carry that?" I offered.

"Please." She handed me the box. Taking two steps away long the soil between the short green wheat, she stopped.

"What you're suggesting…" She whipped at her eyes with her sleeve, shaking her head.

"My Kazu…"

***

That night, Dan the Baby went to bed with Roadkill at his feet. Bill sat at his side in the rocker, holding the wonderful picture book, *Go, Dog. Go!* Ali and I were in the doorway, listening to the story, watching Bill kiss his son goodnight and turn off the lamp.

Backing out into the hall, Ali offered me Kazu's room.

"It's our only spare." Her voice was kind and caring. Her distant gaze said differently.

"I'll take the couch if that's okay?"

Without looking inside Kazu's bedroom, I knew it would be as he had left it last.

"Sure. Let me get you some bedding."

Bill had disappeared. He had been quiet all evening, a polite smile given when necessary.

"Help yourself to the kitchen." Ali brought me the bedding. "Midnight snack or whatever. I know you don't sleep well."

"Thank you," I said, "and I apologize."

"Accepted. Next time you visit, I hope it's for a better reason."

She kissed my cheek and walked away, turning off lamps one after the other.

***

An hour after Bill and Ali went to bed, I sat on the couch beside my pillow and folded blankets. There was a message from Rhonda that I had ignored until I was alone. Adjusting the volume to low, I tapped Play.

"Pie, that Lieutenant De Los Santos called me. He whispered the voicemail. The Puerto Mita detectives have a fresh lead on Jappy, convinced he had some part in that hotel killing. They're starting to suspect that the boy also made off with a large sum of money after the airport murder. They are close to tying the two events together. He didn't understand how. While the boy got away, they are confident he'll raise his head and surface.

"In other news, that creepo-matic reporter sent over the first batch of files and notes. There's nothing in them that didn't make the papers—what a waste of time and money. I'm not wiring him another dime until he agrees to share his photographs. The sack of shat is dancing around that. Wants twelve k for them. With your say so, if he comes through, I'll wire the funds in the morning.

"I hope you're enjoying Bill and Ali and their little boy. It must be great to hang with them for a bit.

"Later."

Hang with them, indeed—me, from a barn rafter.

Rhonda's latest was encouraging. When it was just her and I on this, I would have been pleased and doing my best thinking on how these latest pieces fit. But there I sat in my son's home, having dropped my bag of puzzle pieces in their laps like I was expecting something other than the sadness and hurt I had delivered.

I stood from the couch and crossed to the backyard window. The rear porch light glowed on their patio furniture and a few feet beyond.

There was my grandson's memorial, the light not reaching it, floating in a concrete sea.

Knowing I couldn't find sleep, I pulled a chair over to the window and sat.

A breeze came in from the fields, and the black silhouette of

Kazu's pirate ship turned on the water. I could have arrived with Christmas presents and holiday cheer. I might have brought love and bad jokes and caring. And what had I done instead?

Sometime later, snow began to fall.

Chapter Eight

Christmas

At six the following morning, Bill had made Dan the Baby's favorite breakfast: pancakes with Fruit Loops stirred into the batter. I sat with them at the kitchen table, Roadkill on my lap, watching Dan the Baby with fond eyes. I was passing on breakfast, drinking another cup of coffee after a sleepless night. Ali knelt before her little boy, lacing up his rubber boots.

"We're headed into town to pick out a Christmas tree." She stood for a bite of toast from the plate beside the sink.

"I'm full," Dan the Baby announced. He climbed from his chair and Ali helped him into his winter coat. I stood as well.

"Let me heat the truck for you," I offered.

"Thank you." She handed me the keys.

The driveway and fields beyond were covered with six inches of snow. Climbing into Ali's flatbed truck, I started the engine and cranked the heat up all the way. Before me was the defrosting ice-glazed windshield. Tired as I was, it suggested a viewfinder impossible to use.

Hearing Ali's boots on the gravel, I climbed out. She opened the passenger door and boosted Dan the Baby into his car seat. Rounding to me, she squeezed my arm and climbed behind the wheel.

"You sticking around for Christmas?" she asked.

"No. I think it best I get on the road."

"Yes. That." She turned to Dan the Baby. "Tell your grandpa that you love him and goodbye."

The child smiled at me and waved, looking delighted and confused. Ali pulled her door closed.

I stepped back as she put the truck in reverse and backed away. Instead of rolling it out onto the long driveway, she put it in park and climbed out. Walking to me, her hand rested on my arm.

"Pie, I know your heart was right, but coming here before you knew anything for sure was wrong."

"I agree. And I am so sorry."

"I know you are. Next time, bring a new wife or something." She let out a slight smile, adding, "We love you."

"I love you, too."

Climbing back into the truck, she drove away with my youngest grandson for a Christmas tree adventure.

Back inside the kitchen, I did the dishes as Bill sat with a cup of coffee, having pulled on his heavy work coat.

"How long are you staying?" he asked.

"I'm heading out this morning."

"If you have to. We'd love to have you for Christmas."

"Yes. Next year for sure."

"Good. So, where's your next stop?"

"A hotel somewhere between here and the border."

"With the weather, it might take you three or more days."

"Yes, can't help that."

"Dad, I don't think you're going to be allowed to take the dog into Mexico."

I hadn't thought of that.

"Can I put a bow on his head?" I asked.

"Dan would love that."

I looked over at Roadkill curled up in the corner. I would

miss him but loved the idea of Dan the Baby's adventures with that adorable dust mop. I took my keys from my pocket, saying, "I think I'll head out early."

"If it can't wait until after Christmas, it can't. Keep me posted, please. Best not to talk to Ali when you call. She's struggling just to accept and move her feet forward."

"Yes, of course."

"I'll walk you out."

"No need."

He opened his arms to me and I stepped into them.

"I appreciate what you're trying to do," Bill said. "Not only for us but for Kazu. I raised him, loved him as my own."

"Yes, you did," my voice was wet. I cleared my throat.

So did Bill.

He spoke next, stepping back.

"Call me if you need anything." His voice was husky. "Let me know what you find, good or bad."

"I will."

Bill got the door for me. "Drive carefully, *Grandpa*." He gave me a wry smile.

"Ouch." I returned the smile and stepped out of the house.

Climbing into the modern and cold Willy, it was like I had stepped back into another life. While it idled and thawed out, wipers running, I looked across to the back porch door. Bill stood in the warm light, watching me, his expression heavy and also strong.

I backed the jeep out onto the field road and started up their driveway, wondering just what in the hell I was doing.

"Missing Christmas to chase a ghost," I rebuked myself. I could stop right there, go back to my son and his family, dig up witty banter, and relax into the holidays with them. I could have and maybe I should have. But I didn't. Thirty minutes later, I found my way to the highway and took the south onramp.

***

The miles rolled by one after another. I wished I had Roadkill to talk to, pleased as I was about his new home with Dan the Baby. The roads were clear, the sky dark and gray, rain and flurries off and on. The wipers swung back and forth, and I let the rhythm and the flat highway hypnotize me; the best way to kill time.

When the fuel gauge was almost to empty, I pulled off for a fill-up. Standing at the pumps, I dialed Rhonda's number.

"How far am I from the border?"

Rhonda laughed. "Would help to know where you are."

"Four hours south of Hutchinson, Kansas.

"Okay. Gimme a sec." She muted the call.

"Okay. If you're on Highway 35 and I don't see how you wouldn't be…"

"I am."

"And how are the roads?"

"Wet. slow."

"Looks like Austin is about halfway. Book you a room?"

"Yes, please. Near the freeway."

While she worked her magic, I entered the minimart for beef jerky and a couple of cans of grape soda. They didn't have Fanta. I was seated behind the wheel when she came back on.

"Got you a Super Eight. You'll be slumming right beside the highway."

She gave me the exit number and address.

"Any other news?" I asked.

"Yes, of course. Some of the mystery unravels. There will be six pages on the hotel fax machine waiting for you."

"You know I can't wait," I whined.

Rhonda enjoyed that. "Thought so. Nothing from that Puerto Mita cop. Most of what I'm faxing you is the second installment of documents from that ass clown reporter. No pictures yet. Some of it is very interesting. He dug pretty deep with his sources among the gang double-crossed at the airport. Brave of him, I'll give him that. Anyway, the boy not only turned his gun on his employer but somehow also cleaned out one of their accounts just before the shat hit the fan. It's not for sure, the reporter repeated, but he also said it was more than enough suspicion for the thugs to want to talk with the boy before he is, as Staines said, *disappeared*."

"He's a twelve-year-old boy. What? A killer and a banker?"

"Resourceful, that's for sure. That reporter offered to sell us the next batch, saying it's all about what happened at that hidden hotel. Should I? As I bet you suspect, the price has gone up. You can afford it..."

"Barely," I added for her. "Yes, buy the files. And press him for the photographs."

"Pierce? For a minute, let's talk about your finances. Have you signed the divorce docs? Any decision on that job offer? You'll get nineteen weeks of the principal shoot. Choice of assistant cameraman. Or think about losing that silly Jeep dealership?"

"Willy dealership."

"That, too."

I looked out across the gas station to the highway, a quarter mile off. Eighteen-wheelers were filling the air with mist as they streamed by, headed south. In a couple of minutes, I would be out there too, racing south as well. They had a destination. I didn't even know how to get to Puerto Mita after I crossed into Mexico. And if and when I got there, what exactly was an ex-cinematographer going to do?

"Pie?"

I shook my head. One step at a time, even if the where and how were unknown.

"I'll look over the divorce papers this evening," I told Rhonda, climbing inside the Willy.

"Really? I won't say it's about time because I didn't think you ever would. Whatever else I find out today, I'll fax along as well."

"Thank you." There were probably questions, a dozen or more, I should be thinking of and asking.

"You be safe, please." Rhonda rang off.

***

South of Marietta, Oklahoma, just before the border into Texas, the Willy conked out. Yes, my brand-new Willy's engine died. I pulled off, smelling smoke. I had enough momentum to coast off the highway and onto a gravel turnout. There was a quarter of a tank left. No warning lights lit the dash. Smoke was filling the interior from under the dashboard.

I climbed out and walked away from the toxic smoke, finding a towing company on my phone. A small flag of flame wavered from under the left front fender. I retrieved my suitcase and briefcase, realizing that whatever had broken wasn't going to get a quick fix. The call was picked up on the fourth ring.

"Three A Towing, mechanical or accident?"

"Mechanical."

"Location?"

"I'm on the side of I35."

"Can you be more specific?"

I knew "dunno" wouldn't work. A hundred yards farther out on the highway was an exit sign. I gave him the road name, adding, "I'm parked back from it."

"Type and color of your vehicle?"

"A white Willy."

"As in a Jeep?"

"Yes."

"We will be there in forty minutes." The dispatcher ended the call.

Gentle snowflakes started to fall. Looking over the turnout, I carried my belongings to an oak tree barren of leaves but offering some protection. A sagging barbwire fence ran the back of the gravel. Beyond was a field of limp grassland running straight and forever. No farmhouse, no marks from tilling. I stood and stared at the Oklahoma flatlands for the next five minutes.

When I turned around, I smelled smoke. Standing with my suitcase at my feet, I called Rhonda.

"I got a problem."

The Willy was engulfed in flames.

***

Three firetrucks arrived, along with the highway patrol. As the Willy was sprayed, it sent up more swirling black oily smoke. The officers joined me under the tree, asking cursory questions about the origin of the fire. I finally got to say, "Dunno." It took twenty minutes to completely put out the fire, leaving my brand-new Willy a blackened shell on melted tires.

The two highway patrolmen left me to talk with the firemen. Waiting for the tow truck, I called Rhonda again.

"Hey ya, I'm going to need a rental."

"Okay. Why?"

"The Willy died."

"Know what killed it? Scratch that, where are you?"

"Stranded here in Frostbite Falls."

"That a real town?"

"Course not. Were you raised without cartoons? A deprived childhood?"

The tow truck pulled in. I read the emblem on the side. "I'm near Thackerville, Oklahoma."

"On it. And by the way, no, we didn't get cartoons in my family. Such stuff was considered subversive."

"I think that's sad. Let's see about getting me a car."

"Right. Gotta ask, did you watch cartoons when you were a kid?"

"No need. I lived in one. Hollywood."

***

I rode with the tow truck guy, the black husk of my Willy on the flatbed at our backs. Thackerville was a few miles up the road, dusted with snow. Three A Towing was located two blocks up Sixth Street, backed up against the airport, inside a fenced-in lot of wrecked and crushed cars and trucks, mostly trucks. The driver tilted the steel bed and winched the Willy to the ground back of their office. After paying for the tow, I asked the man behind the desk where the nearest car rental shop was.

"That's easy. Two doors down."

I thanked him, picked up my two cases, and went back out into the light falling snow. The Thrifty Car Rental was a glass shoebox set on top of a brick trim. Hoping it was the one Rhonda had booked, I walked up the sidewalk to it and went inside. I was in a town maybe one-fifth the size of Dent, and had to wait in line. A woman in a long butterscotch cashmere coat and a matching hat was first in line, the clerk behind the counter typing, looking at a monitor.

While waiting, I looked out front. Evening was darkening the sky. *The car first, then some sleep*, I thought. *Get on the road again at dawn*. I overheard the clerk explain, "I'm sorry, ma'am, our last car is booked. A reservation came in before you did."

Ten to one that would be me. Thank you, Rhonda.

"Bet the casino has cars," the clerk offered, raising an uncertain smile.

"Thanks bunches, hon, but it's snowin' out there, and I ain't in a hoofing mood."

"Ma'am, I'm sorry." The clerk leaned to the side and finger-waved me forward. The woman wearing expensive cashmere stepped to the side along the counter, taking out her phone.

I stepped forward, gave the clerk my name, and took out my wallet. While the paperwork was being printed, I overheard the woman at my side say, "I'm stranded, that's why. I'm sorry. Not sure what to do."

During the pause, my paperwork was placed in an envelope and handed over, along with the keys.

"There's no need to yell at me." The woman at my side held her phone from her ear.

Looking at the key fob, I saw that the last available car was a Buick Regal.

"Yes, my mistake. I'll figure it out… somehow." The woman turned and gazed at me. She had sad eyes and a beautiful face: honey-colored skin, black eyes, expressive red lips, a delicate thin nose.

"I'm not confused," her voice was halting, hesitant.

I took up my suitcase and briefcase and started to turn for the door.

"I know I'm lost." She looked like she might cry. Her lovely dark eyes welled with tears. A second later, that changed, and there was hissing anger; her gaze narrowed, her lips pulled back from her perfect white teeth.

"Because I'm stuck here in bum-fuck Oklahoma," she growled.

Oh, I liked that. Fiery, even when troubled. No quitter there.

Placing my back to the glass door, I pushed it open. Cold, wet air rushed in. Her lovely face was almost familiar, like I had seen her in profile at some point in life.

"No, I, I apologize." She had turned on a dime to sincere repentance. I admired the quick change of mind and heart, attracted to the complexity, like that of my soon-to-be ex-wife.

She was stranded. I made a quick call.

"Would you like a ride?" I offered.

She appeared to notice me for the first time; studying me with cool disinterest, my face first, then down my body, slowly. Her eyes returned to mine.

"Are you creepy?" she asked.

"Don't think so."

Her beautiful eyes calculated fast. She ended the call without another word, offering me a smile, a true heartbreaker.

"Where ya headed?" she asked.

"I'm done with the roads for the day."

"Where ya staying?"

"That's my next call." I would call Rhonda from the road.

"I suggest the casino."

"Here in Thackerville?"

"Yep. It's a big deal, for Oklahoma, anyway. A lift would be great if ya don't mind."

We went out into the cold evening, snow falling on the parking lot. I opened the passenger door for her. As she climbed in, I stashed my things in the back seat.

"Maxine. Max, if ya like," she held her hand out as I climbed in behind the wheel.

"Pierce, or Pie, if ya please," I tried out her accent and failed and grinned. She took the rental car folder from the dash and opened the courtesy map.

"Hon, I'll get us there if you'll just keep us on the pavement."

I agreed and steered us out onto the street.

"Turn left, please."

I did, turning the wipers to a faster pace. They were sweeping slush. We rolled to the end of the block. On the corner was a used car lot. Mostly very used cars, all old and worn and road beaten, except a filthy gray Jaguar, its hood up. All the vehicles for sale looked like they had been waiting for a home for a long, long time.

"Was tempted to buy a car," Maxine said, "but I'm all tapped out."

Stopping at the intersection, I glanced at her, seeing that her makeup was film-set perfect, subtle, accenting her beauty.

There were no other cars anywhere. The stop sign was a waste of time.

"Where ya headed tomorrow?" she asked.

"Puerto Mito in Mexico."

"Lordy, no. What a filthy country. You sure?"

"I am."

"Getting yourself a tropical vacation?"

"Not this time. I'm looking for someone."

"A lost lover?"

"Far from that. I'm trying to find a boy."

"I'll ask again. Are you creepy?"

I shook my head with a grin. She purred a soft, husky laugh.

"Where are you headed?" I asked.

"I'm headed for sleep. I've spun up a real mess. My brain needs unplugging." She tapped the map in her lap, adding, "A mile up, take a right."

"Are you from the area?" I took another look before focusing on the road. Her midnight black hair was silky smooth from what had to be a thousand brush strokes.

"Ok-la-hom-a? God forbid. I'm a Texan. I was headed home to finish torching the last of my marriage. What's your story?"

I liked her free and random way with words. So I went with the same.

"I'm a retired camera monkey, getting divorced, in search of a twelve-year-old who might be my grandson…and a serial killer."

"Do I have to ask a third time?" She had a lovely sandpaper laugh.

"You're what?" she asked. "A bounty hunter? A po-lice man?"

"Neither. What I am is a confused and uncertain… Grandpa."

She smirked at my struggle with that last word.

"Your story?" I asked.

"Protect my holdings. That worthless Brit. Shark without a heart. We had ourselves a brief and tidy marriage. That's out the door, and he's at my money in a hundred different ways. Seriously for a sec, I'm frightened."

"He doesn't want the divorce?"

"Oh, he's fine with that as long as he can back up a truck

and steal me blind. What love-struck me didn't see was his cruel and raging mind. He's taken more than a couple of swings at me, missing *most* of the time."

I looked at her, seeing her lovely neutral gaze turned to the storm we were driving into.

"We need to turn there." She pointed up the road to the upcoming intersection.

"Good of you to get away," I said, the words sounding lame. I turned on the blinkers.

"Got one good thing out of it all, a Dixie plate full of English slang from that *queer ol' nut job.*"

I laughed. So did she.

"You're really after a grandson who might also be a killer?"

"Maybe, if it's him. I'm trying to figure that out."

"But you're headed south, anyway. Running with the hunch. I admire that."

"Thank you."

I made the turn, feeling her beautiful eyes on the side of my face.

"Looks like the casino is about ten minutes from here," she said softly, not looking down at the map, continuing to look to me. "I can see it already. All tinseled and gaudy lights and bells ringing everywhere."

"And the haunted and dead pulling levers."

"Ex-act-ly." She sounded pleased, her mood again turning on a dime.

Outside the cocoon of the car, the snow was falling harder. I turned on the headlights, and dancing flakes fell slowly through the beams. She studied the map for the rest of the drive, and I did my best to keep us on the pavement.

When we rolled in under the concrete awning before the casino, two employees in gold Win Star vests and black pants swarmed the Buick from both sides. A young valet offered to open my door.

"Don't' waste time with that," she suggested. "I'll betcha you can save a twenty and navigate to the parking spot."

I climbed out, put my bags on the curb to be taken inside, telling the valet, "I got the car." Then, with a shrug and a smile, I added, "She knows best."

His eyes rose from the keys in my hand, his smile indifferent.

I found us a spot in the underground lot near the elevators. She touched my arm as I parked the car.

"I've decided, just so ya know."

"Decided what?" I asked.

"You're not *dangerously* creepy."

"Thank you. I bet you're about done with today."

"Oh, hell yes. All I want is a room and a big clean bed. Sleep away the ugly thoughts."

"Same here, after I make few calls."

"Your mysterious pursuit."

"My mysterious pursuit."

Walking beside her, I noted for the first time since meeting at the car rental agency that she had no luggage, only a tiny cocktail purse.

We rode the elevator up to the lobby and walked side by side to the front desk. The air was warm and filled with bells dinging among the strands of an upbeat Seventies pop song.

The concierge met us a few feet from the counter, apparently delighted to escort us the next five feet.

"Welcome to the Win Star. If there is anything—"

"Sleep," Maxine cut in. "Deadened, lovely sleep is all."

"Yes, we..." he stammered. "Of course."

I stepped to the counter. "We both need rooms, please," I told the young woman before me.

Five minutes later, she placed two room keys on the spotless granite. I paid for mine, and Maxine did the same.

Having looked Maxine and me over with smiles and pleasantries, the receptionist assigned us adjoining rooms that neither of us had requested. A youth in a gold vest offered to take my bags up.

"Thank you," I said.

Maxine's grinned and shook her head but didn't chide.

We parted in the hall. My door was already open with my bags just inside. I tipped the young man a ten-dollar bill and he departed.

"Sleep well," I offered Maxine.

"Good luck with your phone calls." She unlocked her door and disappeared inside.

With the briefcase open on the foot of the bed, I pulled a chair over before it and took out my phone.

"Hey ya," I said when Rhonda answered.

"Hello, Pierce." Her voice was neutral.

"Hello, Pierce? Where's hey ya, Pie, how's tricks?"

"Tricks? Where did that come from? You enter a time warp?"

"What's wrong?" I asked.

"Had a scary call from Rex from Brownsville, Texas, the fake U.S. Marshal."

"Our lisping cowboy?"

"That be him. One and only. By the way, where are you?"

"In a casino near Thackerville."

"Why would a town named Thackerville have a casino? Scratch that. Give me the fax number there."

I read it off to her from a card on the dresser behind me.

"Good. Go get the docs and call me back."

Five minutes later, I called her.

"Got them?" Rhonda answered.

"Right in front of me."

"Look at page five."

I flipped through the pages of the second installment from our greedy reporter, Carson Staines.

"What am I looking for?"

"Second paragraph. See the name Quinteros? According to

Staines, that's the man running *Nuestra Familia*. Looked it up. It means "our family." They're the ones hunting for Jappy."

"How does our Rex from Texas fit in?"

"He didn't say, of course, but surely he's working for them."

"Why would this *family* hire someone in the States if the boy is in their country?"

"Best question yet. I don't know the answer, but we're gonna figure that out. Now, the other thing."

"What other thing?" I looked down. With the phone between my shoulder and jaw, my hands had formed a viewfinder all on their own.

"Just before he hung up on me…"

"Yes?"

"My next call is to that worthless Lieutenant De Los Santos. See what he has on *Nuestra Familia…*"

"Rhonda? What did this Rex say to you?"

"He said, 'This is simple. Stop. We know where you live. We know where your parents live as well.'"

***

Rhonda and I talked about what she had to do for her safety and that of her parents. She agreed to let me hire one of the many Hollywood security companies and promised to make that her next call. When we ended the call, I raised the viewfinder my hands had formed. Instead of the collage of facts and the unknowns about the boy, there were faces; some well-known, others masked.

I called her back and hit voicemail and said:

"Drop everything. No more digging, no more calls to these whack jobs. You're going to step away, immediately. I want you to call me as soon as security is in place. Thank you for everything you found, but we're done. Promise me."

Chapter Nine

Burn After Reading

I choose to take a shower to chase away the bats in the attic, much like I guessed Maxine did with sleep. Sitting beside my open briefcase on the bed, I absently flipped through the room service menu. I don't recall what I ordered and ate.

Too early for bed, there was a placard on top of the television listing the available films. An hour-plus of immersion would be a fine way to continue avoiding the mystery. I saw that a Coen brothers' film was available, *Burn After Reading*. Cinematography was by a pal, Emmanuel Lubezki. For the length of the movie, I was captivated by the camerawork and compositions, pallet choices and lighting.

After reading the scrolling credits all the way to "The End," I knew I had to turn the chair around. No more distractions. Removing the files and sliding the briefcase aside, I laid them out in chronological order. There before me were the clippings, the few photographs and maps, the faxes from Rhonda and my own notes. A story of sorts, a beginning without an ending, starting with the sad first newspaper articles about the airplane crash.

What did the files say to me? Nothing new, factually.

Rhonda called to say that there was now security parked in

front of her and her parent's homes.

"Good. You heard my message?" I asked.

"Yes. Hate it but will do."

"Promise?"

"I faxed you before I heard your voicemail."

"Rhonda?"

"Yes, I promise. For now."

"Thank you."

With Rhonda and her mom and dad safe and not knowing or caring what time it was, I climbed into the bed, not bothering to gather up the files. Having decided to press on alone, I lay there, hoping sleep would carry me away.

***

Just before midnight, there was a knock on the adjoining door. I got up and unlocked it, and there was Maxine in a black camisole and nothing else.

"How did your mysterious calls go?" she asked.

"Where do I begin? How was your sleep?"

"Productive. Erased most of my worries. A drink?"

She was holding a green bottle of Tanqueray, two tall glasses, and a bucket of ice.

"I don't drink."

"Shame. I do. Can I come in?"

"Yes, of course," I stepped aside, watching her place the bottle, glasses, and ice on the table at the window.

"Anything new about the boy that might be your grandson?"

"Not really, except for a nasty threat."

"Who from?"

I watched her walk away from the liquor on the table. She made it look natural. People who aren't alcoholics can do that. She sat on the edge of the bed and slid the briefcase over to make room.

"The thugs, at least that's what I'm calling them," I answered.

"Why would they threaten you?"

"Because they also want to find him. He agreed to do something and didn't. These are some really scary people. Involved in drug shipping over the border."

I sat on the chair facing the bed.

"Know what I'd do?" she reached over and took my hand. "Write them a big fat check for the boy. Money talks with thugs."

I thought about that. It would be a good idea to talk over with Rhonda, except I couldn't.

"I Googled you," Maxine said. "Hope ya don't mind?"

"Far as I know, that's a first, except for an occasional film school student."

"How would you know?"

"They follow up by sending me questions. Mostly about composition and lens."

"You're married to Pauline Place? That's impressive."

"*She* is certainly impressive. A wonder, if you don't already know. We're divorcing." My eyes returned to the table under the window.

"But you're still married to her?"

"Barely." I shook my head and turned my eyes to her.

"Barely enough for you to still write a great big check?"

"*If* she and I talked, probably. *If* I knew for sure the boy is my grandson. Pauline's done with my years of half-baked antics. I need to think on that."

"Know what I need?" Maxine asked. "And I betcha you do, too."

Raising my hand and placing it on her warm tummy, she leaned for a kiss. I saw and I felt what was beginning. I met her halfway, looking into her lovely, drowsy eyes. Her other hand smoothed up my shoulder to my neck. We kissed deeply. I closed my eyes to the taste of her warm and wonderful wet lips.

She loved me like the strangest of Halloweens.

***

Maxine woke me in the middle of the night, whispering, "Another round of romper room?"

Her warm shoulder and tousled hair were inches from my face. I breathed perfume from her skin and closed my eyes. Her hips pressed back into me. Half-awake, I cupped and caressed her breast, too lost to answer.

"Whatcha think?" she said softly, her legs parting slowly.

"About romper room? I'm in."

"Almost, yes," she purred, her voice husky, her hand reaching back, gliding up my thigh, "I meant about the bribe."

The question was odd, considering what we were beginning to do. My thoughts were scant, at best. Finally, I gathered enough of my wits to say, "I'm not sure."

"Sounds like a probably no." She welcomed me inside her.

Our lovemaking was unlike earlier in the night; more perfunctory, satisfying both of us physically without her endearments.

When I woke, the curtains were filled with gray morning light. Maxine was gone, the adjoining door closed. She had taken the alcohol, glasses, and ice bucket with her.

The bed was in disarray, the blanket and sheets tangled, some of the files still at the foot, most of them spilled onto the floor. Before I took a shower, I gathered them up and stacked them inside the briefcase on top of the FedEx divorce parcel. I looked to the table, foolishly wondering if she had left me a note.

After two cups of coffee from the courtesy Keurig by the sink, I carried my two cases out into the hall. Turning to knock on Maxine's door, I saw it was open, blocked by a room service cart. I knocked on the doorframe.

"Excuse me, do you know when she left?" I asked.

The house cleaner leaned from the bathroom, fresh towels in hand, "Check with the front desk."

I crossed the lobby, asked for my faxes, and paid my bill. With the latest and likely last pages of orderly notes from Rhonda inside the briefcase, I took the elevator down to the parking lot.

What to make of my behavior with Maxine? One-nighters were far from anything I had ever been tempted by. I had never strayed during my marriage, never even thought of it. But last night, I had, no matter that my marriage was "barely" breathing.

"Another time to think about that." I pushed Maxine and the knock on the adjoining door away. I had miles to make, a whole lot of time behind the wheel before I entered Mexico. There would be hours to think up ways to continue the search without Rhonda's assistance.

Private investigator? crossed my mind as I walked up the row I had parked the rental in.

The car looked strange before it was entirely in view. It seemed too low to the ground. Setting the suitcase down behind it, I saw why. All four tires were flat. Tiny shards of broken glass were sprayed along both its sides, the windows bashed in. The hood was up. Vandalized? No, it was worse. The Buick had been murdered.

***

Hotel security called in the report to the Thackerville police. A report was filed over the phone. In the scheme of things, a battered rental car was not a high priority. I called the number on the rental agreement and let them know. The concierge came downstairs to take a look and offered to assist me with a replacement. An hour later, I was behind the wheel of another Buick Regal, this one both shiny and midnight blue.

Jumping onto Highway 35 again, I drove south, trying to figure out if the damage to the rental had been random or personal. It seemed paranoid to believe it was the latter, so I turned my thoughts to the important question. How best to find that boy in the coastal cities of Mexico?

Without Rhonda to lean on for research and advice, I decided to figure out how to use my phone to search for a private detective. Rather than fumble with it while driving the wet and windy highway, I decided to do so the next time I stopped to fill the tank.

The rain was relentless, but at least it wasn't ice or snow. The hours passed. While refueling the car, I had little luck with my clumsy attempts to do an internet search for private detectives in the Puerto Mita area. I scribbled down a few numbers to call when I got a motel that night. Questions for the private investigator came to me.

"Get help contacting the family of thugs."

"Find out how much they want, assuming I can buy them off."

That brought forth the next two decisions.

"Sign the divorce papers and use the proceeds,"

"Free Kazu, if it's him, and somehow sneak him out of Mexico." Yes, I was talking to myself out loud.

I made it as far as Schertz, Texas, just north of San Antonio, before the need for help was shouting at me. After getting a room at a Best Western, I opened the briefcase on the foot of the bed like the night before and called the first number on the list of private detectives.

I spoke with three before calling Carlo "Buzz" Guzman. He answered my call with, "Buzz Guzman Investigations, both sides of the border." His accent was more Texan than Mexican.

I chose him because he was up to date on the *disease*, as he put it, of children working as killers for the drug gangs and, as he described it, the Jappy the Killer story. His English was good, and his retainer was only mildly over the top, three thousand dollars, U.S.

"I'm looking for help finding that boy called Jappy the Killer," I said.

"Call me Buzz, please, and tell me why you are hunting down that particular killer?"

"I believe he's my grandson."

"From the States? You joke, right? Jappy the Killer is American? Haven't heard that one."

"If it's him, yes. That's part of what I would hire you for."

"And how do you think he got down here and involved with… his current career?"

"There was a plane crash outside of Puerto Mita. Supposedly, no survivors, but I think he did. Somehow."

"Excuse me, Mr. Danser, but that's a big somehow."

"Pierce, please. And yes, it is unlikely, but there are photographs, unfortunately, none of his face. And this Jappy, as he's called, has been killing in that same area. There's even a reporter who's been chasing him—"

"Along with many others."

"Yes. I am in talks with the reporter to buy his notes and hopefully photographs too."

"This reporter's name?"

"Carson Staines."

"I've read him, of course. Another ex-pat cranking out bloody trash and bashing Mexico."

"Yes, that's him. He's interviewed the boy. Unfortunately, I don't have those notes yet."

"I bet this hack is suddenly expense. If it is your grandson, what is his name?"

"Kazu."

"Really?"

"I kid you not."

"This Jappy, excuse me, Kazu as you say, is most effective. Smart and creative. Snakes up close, pulls the trigger, and poofs. He likes his disguises. At the airport kill, he was done up as a drooling invalid in a wheelchair, getting right up close."

"He was, *is*, as you say, creative, yes."

"Pierce, I'll be upfront with you. This twelve-year-old grandson with a strange name is in a world of hurt. Senor Quinteros and his gang want him in a big way. He'll be killed and tossed to the side of the road, of course, after they torture him for the location of the money he somehow stole."

That set me back.

"Unless we find him first," I said.

"It would be a big job, but it is possible. If it helps reassure you, I'm known as Buzz because I have my ear inside the snake pits on both sides of the law."

"Good. When could you start?"

"Here's what I can do for you and, yes, I can start immediately. I'll push aside trying to confirm his identity. You can work that while I focus on where they are searching, what Quinteros knows. By the way, any plans to come on down?"

"I'm on my way."

"Not necessary, but that'll be helpful. I might need you to work the American consulate if we decide to legally get him out of the country: my recommendation, a charter flight with your grandson hidden in the back. If the policia get wind of what we're up to, they're going to grab him fast. We don't want him in their hands."

Another series of images could form a collage if I allowed.

"It's an interesting case," Buzz continued. "Complicated, to say the least. I am up to it if you're fully funded."

I paid his retainer with my bank card, and we ended the call.

That evening, I sat before the files spread out on the bed, reading and sorting to no new ideas or insights. I felt untethered without Rhonda at my side, so to speak, and relieved that she had agreed to step away from all this. She had a whole other life and her parents to protect. Briefly, thoughts of Maxine sauntered into my mind, and I quickly buried them. Who needs regret and confusion over a one-night mistake? Dinner was in some chain restaurant a half-mile away. Returning to my room, I showered and climbed into the bed with a last look at my phone for new messages. There were none.

Early the following day, I walked out into a different world. No more rain and menacing dark clouds. In their place was a baby blue sky and pressing heat from a brilliant sunrise. Being a little more than two hundred miles from the border, I found highway maps of Mexico in the next gas station. Measuring with my fingers, it was roughly eight hundred and some miles to Puerto Mita. But first, I had to cross the border.

"What are their roads like?" I worried briefly.

"One step at a time."

I placed my phone on the dashboard, hoping Buzz Guzman would call with progress. Over the next four hours, it was just me and my thoughts, and I admit, some fear—not the best of company. Could Buzz and I find him? Get him out? Get him home? And, of course, was the boy Kazu?

Chapter Ten

Laredo

I arrived in the border town of Laredo, Texas, just after noon, Highway 35 still leading the way.

A mile from the border, the homes and shops with adobe-colored tiles looked tired and worn out. I pulled in at the Palenque Grill restaurant and parked off to the right in the last spot. With my road map of Mexico and the briefcase, I walked through the heat and hazy air, tasting of dust.

I was shown a table and ordered. Out the window, Laredo in the afternoon was in a torpor of slow cars and trucks rolling south in traffic.

The map showed that I would be crossing the Rio Bravo River over the central Gateway Bridge. After I crossed, I had those eight hundred miles to Puerto Mita. Setting the map aside, I opened the briefcase and took out the six pages of Carson Staines notes, starting with article drafts. Jeez, it was pure Hollywood tripe:

Caron Staines
Photojournalist
May 9th, 2018
Draft: Jappy el Niño Asesino
Puerto Mita, Mexico

Jappy the Killer fell from the sky like a fallen angel of death.

Landing in the squalor and crime-infested back streets of Puerto Mita, he began his climb upward, clawing his way through the street gangs. Stealing, fighting, maiming, he rose through the ranks to when a pistol was put in his hand. Thus, began a series of murders, guided by his employers, each more gruesome than the last. Rivals were killed in hotel lobbies, restaurants, and the backstreets; the twelve-year-old sidling up, often as a busboy or beggar, seemingly innocent and sad—until he took his trademark 9mm from his waistband.

By my count, there were five murders before his infamous double cross at the Puerto Mita airport, this bloody killing from a wheelchair in the crowded terminal!

Caron Staines
Photojournalist
Notes from the only meeting with Jappy:
Isla Negra, off the coast of Matamoros

I tracked him to the remote island, Isla de Marionettes, where he was hiding out to let the dust die if it would.

The boy was naturally suspicious of me. Our conversation was brief. (Note: this was the meet where I snapped the photograph of his back—he smartly turned as soon as I raised my camera). His voice is strange. No hint of Spanish or Japanese as his face suggests. More of a flat Midwest American accent. Of course, he wouldn't talk about his past, so I've no idea (yet) where he really came from. Also curious is how he travels. A single backpack contains his life. Of course, I went through it quickly when he was distracted. Art supplies—he draws comic books (!), and he had an old Nokia flip-phone. Nothing more. That day, he wore brown work boots, a black shirt and shorts, and a beat-up baseball cap. We talked for twenty minutes there in his squatter's camp before he became alarmed and ran off into the trees. I was left with the impression of a cunning, cold-hearted killer free of remorse.

All the best qualities of an assassin.

Note: Nice line / possible Header: "Where is Jappy now? There's plenty of wet work for an innocent-looking twelve-year-old with a 9mm."

I stopped reading. Since he was five or six, the Kazu I knew loved to tell stories with ink and pastel pencils. That and his baseball cap.

I put the reporter's notes back inside the briefcase. Digging deeper, I found the one-page Rhonda had sent with "Contacts" typed across the top. There was Carson Staines number. I wanted to talk with this reporter first, then check in with Buzz Guzman. I patted my pocket. The phone was still in the car. Drinking off one of my two glasses of ice water, I headed out into the midday heat to the rental.

Three young women in leather skirts, black boots, and halter tops stood before the Buick. One was squatting with a laptop, another holding a black box at the driver's door. A third girl was on lookout, watching me with hard, confident eyes. Her daring gaze never strayed from me. She spoke to two others in a hushed voice.

"What's going on?" I asked.

"What you think, *puta*? Breaking into this car."

I knew enough Spanish to understand she had called me a *slutty girl.*

I walked past her for the other two: the girl with the laptop and the other kneeling, reaching under the Buick. That was my foolish mistake.

I never saw it coming. A board? A pipe? The butt of a gun?

Struck in the head from behind, I went down hard and fast. Landing on my hands and knees, I turned in time to see a pointed black cowboy boot flying at my face. Stunned and stupid, my head a pulsing flare of pain, I tried to rise, staggered, and fell flat, having just enough wits to curl up. I don't know how long they were it, kicking, cursing, and somehow worse, laughing at the end.

I lay there on the gritty pavement, first hearing the voices of worried restaurant customers and eventually an approaching siren. My bell was rung and still tolling; I let a stranger help me first to my knees and then to my feet.

This kind young man assisted me back across to the restaurant's front door and inside the wonderfully cool air. I saw that my lunch had been served as he helped me sit. I stared at it, dumbfounded, headache screaming. I drank off the second glass of water, coughed up spit and blood and wiped my mouth with a napkin. The police siren stopped wailing out front. I was grateful for that. My table was circled by restaurant workers and curious customers, talking among themselves and not to me, which helped. I stared at my meal, perhaps in shock, undoubtedly confused. It had been a fast explosion of violence, leaving me with one eye blackened and swollen, my ribs and back screaming, my hands scraped and cut. Had I fought back? I doubted it.

A fresh glass of water was set on the table.

"Thank you," I managed, my tongue thick.

As I drank, a policewoman sat down across from me. She was blonde, green-eyed, tight jawed, and looking at me with more suspicion than concern. She took out a pen and pad.

"What happened out there?" she asked.

"I got the hell kicked out of me," I stated the obvious.

"Your name and ID, please."

I handed her my wallet.

Pushing my napkin into the glass of water, I wiped my face. My nose and forehead and right cheek were scraped and bloody.

"What started the fight… Mr. Pierce Danser?"

"I interrupted them."

"Them?"

"Three girls. I went out to get my phone, and they were breaking into my car."

"I see, and what happened next?"

I extended my arms out to my sides for display.

"The three girls attacked you?" she asked.

"Worse. The girls attacked me and won big time."

That got me a slight, sympathetic smile.

"If it helps, they didn't get in," the officer said.

"I'm thrilled."

She wrote for a minute before looking across.

"You're driving a rental. Business or pleasure?"

"Certainly not pleasure."

"I hope you're not planning on crossing the border."

"And why's that?" I put down the soggy napkin.

"Mr. Danser, you can't take a rental car into Mexico."

I didn't know that. My aching mind went to work at half-speed at best.

"Where are you staying?" the officer asked.

I ignored that. I looked at her chest badge.

"Officer Kendrick, do you know where there's a Jeep dealership?"

***

I stayed at my table in the restaurant for another hour, nursing my wounds and drinking ice water. Customers came and went. I made a list of what I needed to do. Officer Kendrick told me there was a Jeep dealership on something called the Bob Bullock Loop. Find that, do a walk-away on the rental, lease a Willy if they had one in stock. Dig out my passport and get in the queue to cross into Mexico.

The list done, I lingered. No, I stalled. Crossing the border was a big step, not in difficulty, but commitment. I wasn't uncertain. I was beaten and alone. A bit of pity nudged, like a sad-looking dance partner, tender hand out. I shook my head gingerly and got up, leaving cash on the table.

Back behind the wheel, I took my phone from the dash.

"You don't have enough wits right now to question the reporter," I decided, dialing my recently-hired private detective. I hit his voicemail and asked Buzz to call me with a status. Turning to the left, away from the border, I started my search for the Bob Bullock Loop. The directions the policewoman had given were hazy, but I did recall her saying the dealership was "Just a way north."

When the cellphone purred and vibrated on the dashboard, my first thought was a foolish hope. Rhonda? Knowing better, I looked at the number and answered.

"Hello, Buzz."

"Hello, Pierce. You sitting down?"

"Why yes, I am."

"Where are you?"

"Laredo. Near the border. On my way to lease a Willy."

"Won't ask why."

I didn't explain what I had learned about taking rental cars into Mexico. Surely, *he* would know that.

"What's up?" I asked.

"Big news. Your bill is going to be ugly."

"Go on."

"No need to drive to Puerto Mita."
"And why is that?"
"He got across somehow. He's in the States."

Chapter Eleven

Louisiana

"What? How? No, where to?" I asked.

"Northern Florida." Buzz sounded very pleased with himself.

"Can you be more specific? I hear it's a long, wide state."

"I'm working that."

"How did you find out?"

"Carson Staines is there."

"Give me a minute. I'll call you back." I ended the call.

I pulled off the road into a quickie mart. Inside, I found a USA map on a rack beside the magazine stand. With the map opened out against the steering wheel, I called Buzz back.

"Damn, I'm good," Buzz answered.

"Yes. Something new?"

"Staines last used his credit card in the Daytona area. I don't know where he's heading. Know how to get there?"

"I'm good. It looks like I go thirteen hundred miles. And turn left."

"Good. It should take you two days. I'm calling him next. You okay with a sizable bribe to loosen his lips?"

"Yes. If he has more photographs, I want them as well," I said.

"On it," Buzz ended the call.

It looked like I could take Highway 59 northeast to Highway 10 that ran across the south to the Florida coast. I could get a motel and start first thing in the morning. It was three in the afternoon with sunset in a couple of hours. I decided to drive on until dark.

Instead, five hours later, I was in the middle of nowhere, crossing the flatlands of Texas. No calls from Buzz. Just me behind the wheel staring off into the headlights revealing the miles.

I wanted the highway to hypnotize me, dull me to a stupor to pass the time. Didn't happen. How could it? Had the boy made it across the border? Alive and well? Surviving how? And, of course, was it Kazu?

Later, I pulled off in Beaumont, Texas to refuel and clean the windshield.

Getting back onto Highway 10, sometime later the road signs said I was close to the Louisiana border and that's when my phone rang.

"Bad news, my friend," Buzz greeted.

"I can take it. I'm renewed."

"Wanna bet? There was an incident in Flagler Beach. It's in all the papers."

"Incident?"

"Our Mr. Staines tried to mow down a bunch of street urchins, driving the sidewalk. Ran over a couple of tourists who got in his way, killing both."

I slumped behind the wheel, confused.

"He what? Why?"

"Police say he was probably on drugs to do such a thing."

"They have him, right. What's he saying?"

"Oh. They have him, but he's not talking. Can't."

"Why?"

"He's dead."

***

Our best source of information on the boy's identity had gone up in flames. Literally. Buzz told me that Carson Staines hit a sidewalk lamppost at a high rate of speed. The car caught fire, and that was the end of his story. The end of that stream of information. Two dead. The street kids rounded up and questioned—no mention of an Asian-looking twelve-year-old.

I drove an hour into Louisiana, where I found a roadside hotel, showered, and climbed into bed. Attempting to find any kind of positive light on the news, I failed. Pulling a pillow over my head, sleep somehow found me.

Chapter Twelve

Alabama

Measuring with my fingers on the map, my reckoning had me about seven hundred miles from Daytona. Back behind the wheel just after sunrise, I turned the Buick onto the on-ramp and out onto eastbound Highway 10.

The hours and miles passed, interrupted by stops for fuel. Highway 10 skirted the underbelly of the South with the Gulf of Mexico somewhere off to my right. I had left Buzz Guzman two voicemails. So far, I hadn't heard back from him.

Just past the southern tip of Alabama, I started across the panhandle of north Florida. An hour along, my phone rang.

"Pierce, it's Buzz. Have pen and paper?"

"No, I'm driving. What's up?"

"Two subjects. First, the dead reporter. With Staines dead, I've been sniffing around the underbelly of Daytona for info on the boy."

"Do you have any contacts with the Daytona police?"

"I'm making some now, but we have to let the dust settle a bit. The killing of that couple has the authorities all in a spin. They've found Staines' sleaze bag hotel, by the way."

"Where are you?" I asked.

"I'm in Daytona. Landed this morning. Where are you?"

"Middle of nowhere on Highway 10. It looks like I'll be there by the middle of the night."

"I'm headed to the wrecking yard as soon as I figure out which one. Sometimes the cops miss stuff, especially when it's in a toasted car. I'm planning to *persuade* the owner to let me have a quick look. Who knows what that lunatic might have been traveling with? Everything's probably in an evidence locker, but it's worth a peek."

"I'd love to get my hands on his laptop."

"Fat chance, but who knows. More likely, they got it from the hotel. Their headquarters is my second stop."

'Is it time for me to go to the police?"

"That's probable, but not just yet. They've already got a real mess on their hands. Now, the second topic."

"Yes?

"Ever hear the name Rex Thurges?"

"The first name, yes. U.S. Marshal, or pretending to be."

"That's him. Another crazed bounty hunter working both sides of the border."

"Did you talk to him?"

"Oh no. I hear he's not the type to chat. I would have to go through layers of the Quinteros gang just to get his number. Frankly, I want to live a long life."

"This guy is a killer?"

"The word in Puerto Mita is that our friend Rex has the Jappy job. And yes, killing can be side work to the bounty business. With a few of them."

Murder a twelve-year-old boy, no matter what he's done. What world was I in?

"And you don't think I should take this to the police?" I asked. "They could find the boy and protect him."

"Eventually, yes. But we have some time. Putting the boy in a cell isn't going to stop them."

"Any idea how close this Rex Thurges is to finding my grandson if it's my grandson?"

"Not exactly, not yet. They might have a second man on that; I don't know."

"Then what is this Rex up to?"

Buzz sucked a deep breath before saying, "They've sent him to persuade you to stop and turn around."

There was silence. I stared up Highway 10, wipers sweeping away the rain.

I heard Buzz's car door open and close, followed by his footsteps.

"Do you know where this Rex is?" I asked.

"Not yet, but soon. One last thing."

"Yes?"

"Ho ho ho."

"Huh?"

"Bro, it's Christmas Eve."

Chapter Thirteen

Merry Christmas

Just before the end of Christmas Eve, I pulled off in Tallahassee to fill the tank. Standing under the blinding fluorescent lights, my eyes stung, my nerves were jittery, and my thoughts were scrambled. I had hundreds of miles to go, no matter how fast I drove.

The minimart attached to the gas station had been decorated for Christmas. Silver tinsel and blinking red and green bulbs surrounded the door and large windows. While the gasoline nozzle vibrated in my hand, I spoke to the lonely silhouette behind the plate glass window a dozen yards away.

"Merry Christmas," I offered.

It's not like the clerk could hear me. He was as isolated as I was. Did he feel a holiday lift and glow? I hoped so. I didn't. I was stuck with a single, painful question.

Where does a twelve-year-old boy on the run celebrate Christmas?

Back out on the endless Highway 10, I pushed down harder on the accelerator. I had hours to go and was determined to shave them.

I had the next hour to myself on the highway except for

passing an occasional long-haul truck obeying the speed limits. My first impression of the Florida panhandle held true—massive pine trees lined the road with wilderness spreading beyond.

Around one in the morning, I slowed up for pair of headlights looking about to pull out onto the highway. When I saw that the car was going to do the sensible thing and wait, I accelerated. As I passed, there was a loud crack. With it, glass sprayed from the passenger window.

I screamed; I admit it.

Ducking low, the Buick swerved. I had instinctively turned the wheel to the left. At eighty miles an hour, the car kicked up gravel before slurring on the grass divider. There was no time to check for injuries—I had to get the car in control. I was off the accelerator, the rear of the car swinging around, wanting to swap ends with the front. Turning into the slide, the rear fender smashed something large—a rock? A tree? I never knew. Whatever it was helped point the Buick in the right direction. A hundred yards along, I was back out on the pavement.

The wind was blowing in from both sides. My window had also been taken out. I didn't feel any injuries. No blood that I could see. My foot when down hard on the accelerator. With no apparent wounds or pain, I wanted a good long distance from that car before I pulled off somewhere to take a good look.

For the next twenty minutes, I watched the mirrors for chasing headlights. I came upon an island of lights— a gas station and restaurant signs. There would be people around in case those headlights appeared: a safe place, an island under fluorescents in the middle of the night in the Florida wilderness.

I went as far as turning on the blinkers.

The Buick was running strong and true, no matter its damages.

I didn't lift. I didn't turn. I had three-quarters of a tank.

The warm, humid air was swirling the interior, and I sat in the middle of that cyclone until the fuel gauge light came on.

Even then, I hadn't made enough distance to feel safe.

This Rex or whoever didn't want me finding the boy, Kazu or not.

I wished I had had the wits to see what kind of car it was before the windows exploded. I had no choice but to refill the tank, so I took the next off ramp with a sky-high gold and blue Sunoco sign.

Pulling in under the harsh sodium lights to the pumps, I had company. A man in his thirties, looking road-weary and exhausted, was filling his minivan's tank. I climbed out, seeing the mound of Christmas packages stacked to the roof in the back area. It looked like three or four children were in the back seats, their heads resting against each other, resembling sweet sleeping angels. The man gave me a wane smile and nod.

"Merry Christmas," he added.

I said the same, offering my tired smile. I circled the Buick before returning to the pump. Besides the missing windows, the only other damage was the crunched in left rear fender.

As the tank filled, I watched the off-ramp for approaching vehicles. A lumbering U-Haul van waddled to the stop sign and turned right for the McDonalds. That was all.

The Christmas travelers departed, heading for the west on-ramp. A couple of minutes later, I followed but turned east.

"Shot at on Christmas," I said to myself as the Buick picked up speed. Ten to one, there's a Country and Western song with that title. That was the only humor for the night. I didn't know where I was except that I was still on Highway 10. Farther on in the night or the morning was Daytona, where the hunt would continue. I spoke to the faceless Rex.

"You're not stopping me. And I'm not turning away."

Part Two

Florida

Let the dogs bark, Sancho. It's a sign that we are on track.

~ Miguel de Cervantes Saavedra

Chapter Fourteen

Fruit Loop Pancakes

I drove over a long arching bridge that spilled down into Daytona Beach. The sun was a glowing tangerine, rising over the Atlantic through warm winter fog. Stretching to the north and south were pastel-painted high-rises and slight glimpses of wonderful white sand beach and the blue ocean.

My phone buzzed.

"Hope I didn't wake you?" Buzz asked.

"Not at all, thanks. I drove straight through. I'm entering Daytona now."

"Good. Welcome to vacationland."

"Any news?"

"Yes. Let's meet for lunch. I've got a morning with the police and another thing to chase down."

"Give me a hint?"

"Sure, I think we're getting inside that reporter."

"Getting inside a dead reporter?"

"So to speak. Let's meet at the Waffle House at noon. It's on South Atlantic. I'm sure I'll have more news by then."

We rang off, and I drove farther to the sea, passing drive-thru liquor stores, pawnshops, abandoned houses, shops, and quick-cash joints. I was clearly on the backside of vacationland. I scanned for a motel that didn't look too run down and didn't find one. Sleep was pulling at me.

Just a few hours. My eyes were stinging, and my body was sagging behind the wheel. Two blocks farther along Speedway Boulevard, I saw an interesting shop and decided sleep could wait a bit longer. Not much, but some.

I pulled off into the strip mall parking lot to buy myself a Christmas gift. The shop was called Buck's Gun Rack, on the sad, worn street behind fun and festive Daytona Beach. Inside the shop, I learned that Florida law requires a three-day cooling-off period, so I left the gun shop with nothing but a box of 9mm hollow points.

Back in the Buick, I drove the rest of the way to the coast. Left or right? I didn't think it mattered. I went left and picked the SeaBreeze Motel a half-mile along. The single-story row hotel was across South Atlantic Boulevard from a wide condo tower. I had no idea how a breeze from the ocean could reach it. The street was like the U.S. border, separating the haves from the never will.

There was no sense locking the car. Its passenger and driver windows were gone, glass pebbles scattered all over the interior. I entered the motel office and got a room, saying, "A few nights at the least."

Key in hand, I retrieved my suitcase and briefcase and started around the swimming pool deck.

The pool was a happening place, no matter the early hour. Two overweight, sunburnt and tattooed couples were poolside, having the drunken time of their lives. Their table under an umbrella was littered with ashtrays and tall bottles of alcohol. They had set out a portable stereo. Their music was all thumping bass, loud enough to loosen tooth fillings. Three children were in the water, completely ignored.

My room was at the end of the row, just off the edge of the

pool deck. The first thing I did was set the alarm clock for three hours of sleep. The room itself was basic, small and worn out.

I needed a shower, but that could wait. First, I had to gather my thoughts and plans.

With the box of bullets and open briefcase at my side on the bed, I formed a viewfinder with my fingers and thumbs. It's sometimes funny how the viewfinders have their own ideas. Instead of the puzzle pieces and fears, I received a Christmas collage of my grandson.

His face, of course, was from the old photograph in my wallet. In it, Kazu was in his pirate boat at home in Kansas. The next vignette was of his mom and dad in the kitchen, laughing until there were tears in Ali's eyes. As had been my style when I was an employed cinematographer, I kept the viewfinder steady before my eyes and spoke to my left, something I also used to do as a kid, alongside Dead Jared, my brother, my once fellow filmmaker.

"Diffuse the left lighting twenty percent."

My imaginary lighting tech did as asked. The composition softened with a kind, amber warmth.

Bill was shaking his head, both surprised and pleased by whatever it was that Kazu had said. I didn't know because the dialogue wasn't coming to me. Ali's arm went around Kazu's shoulder and she pulled him close. All three were delighted with each other. Kazu leaned to his little brother, Dan the Baby, and kissed his forehead, and I received the only spoken line, the younger version of the boy I was hunting, saying, "Merry Christmas, Danny-o."

I spoke to my right side, to the lead audio woman, "Give me the theme music, please."

The soundtrack began, melodic, soft, and swaying.

The loving family of four chatted and laughed.

Bill got up from the table. Kazu greedily took his chair, his father pretending to scowl. Kazu leaned to his baby brother, who was wide-eyed and smiling, looking a little deranged as only infants can.

I knew breakfast would be juice and Fruit Loop pancakes. After breakfast, the family would pad out to the family room to the Christmas tree and presents.

I wanted to stay, to watch the entire film play. One of the occasional hazards of camerawork is the sense of intruding. With a pain in my heart, I pulled my hands apart. The living, breathing collage dissolved, tiny fragments of colorful pieces falling like Michigan snow.

I showered and climbed into the bed. Three hours wasn't much but would have to do. Refresh the brain with slumber so I could get back on the trail.

Chapter Fifteen

7-Eleven

I found the Waffle House on South Atlantic and took a table near the rear. While waiting for Buzz Guzman to show, I looked over the colorful plastic menu. Where else can you get chicken and waffles? I took out my phone and tapped on Rhonda's phone number.

It being Christmas day, I wasn't surprised she didn't answer. I hit voicemail and left a message. "Hey ya, and Merry Christmas. I hope you and your parents are safe and well? Presents and eggnog and all that good cheer. All is good here. I'm still on the hunt and getting real close. Thank you as always for all your help, and I'm glad you're safe."

Hitting send, I looked to the door. No news customers entering. There was a second call that I wanted to make to my wife, Pauline Place. But to say what? "Merry Christmas for the last time?" Once our sons were grown, Pauline and my Christmas tradition was a long swim followed by a meal of pastries in bed. I put the phone down on the table.

Looking out the window, I wondered again how the boy I believed to be Kazu was spending the day.

The tiny bells over the door jingled, and a well-dressed man entered, saw me, and walked my way. He was an enviably tan and handsome man in a cream linen suit, buttoned-up blue shirt, and sand-colored military boots. "Buzz" also described his haircut except for the half-inch flattop you could park a soda can on. He carried a black object held out from the side of his suit coat.

"Pierce," he said, not questioning, walking over and sliding into the booth across from me.

"Good to meet you," I replied.

"Brought you a present, but you can't open it yet." He set a charred laptop on the Formica. Bits of black dust littered the table.

Awe, gee, Buzz, thank you, but I didn't get you anything, came to mind, but humor didn't fit the vibe. His gray eyes were steady on mine, his expression patient and tired.

"That from Carson Staines?" I asked.

"From his trunk, yes. Cost you two hundred to the wrecking yard to walk away with it. It slid under the melted driver's seat."

"Well done. Does it still work?"

"Haven't tried. I have an appointment with this techie in Ponce Inlet, says he does computer autopsies or, as he put it, data extraction from damaged discs."

"It would really help to get his files. And photographs."

"Don't know, but the tech sounded confident."

Our waitress walked up to the table.

"Merry Christmas, guys. Whatcha having?"

Buzz ordered breakfast instead of lunch. Waffles, sausage, and orange juice. That sounded as good as anything, so I ordered the same.

"Have you been watching the news?" Buzz asked as the waitress walked away.

"Not yet. What are they saying?"

"Carson Staines was a nut job. Recent history of strange behavior. Trashy hotels, nearly broke. All indications are of obsession or madness. They're contacting the newspapers he worked for to get more on him, but all his recent articles were about his hunt for Jappy, as he called the boy."

"They say anything about… the *boy* being at the scene, on that sidewalk?"

"No. there were a bunch of kids there; two were injured. Most of the talk was about the death of the couple Staines ran over, and that's who they suspect he was after. No clue why. If you're thinking of talking to the kids, forget it. No names given, of course, they're minors."

"The couple. Could they have been helping the boy?"

"It's remotely possible, but I think they were just in the way. Wrong place, wrong time. They were from Ontario. Snowbirds with some terribly bad luck. I think our best avenue is this bounty hunter, Rex Thurges."

"Do we know where he is? Who hired him?"

"No and no. I've dug up as much as possible on him. He was a U.S. Marshal seven years back. He was fired for malfeasance and beating the crap out of an escapee. His name is known with law enforcement and my sources in the gangs on both sides of the border. More speculation than facts, but the chatter is he's both a tracker and a killer. I did learn that he sometimes partners with another person, which is uncommon."

"Do you have any recent photographs of this Rex?"

"Course not." Buzz looked saddened.

"Any way we can reach him? Offer to buy him out or something?"

"Just reaching him would be a miracle. As far as buying him off, not likely. That would be a terrible move on his part—career-ending. So I think our next best move is this." He drummed his fingers on the laptop.

Our food arrived. Buzz ate slowly, eyes up, pondering. I ate a half sausage and drank my orange juice before sliding my plate aside. Placing cash on the table on top of the bill, I slid off my seat.

"Thank you," I said. "I hope the computer guy can work magic."

"You're welcome. Where you off to?"

"That sidewalk where Staines ran those people over. Not sure why."

"Not a bad idea. It might say something to you. After I drop off the computer, I'm headed back to the police station. Got a detective who doesn't seem to mind a few questions."

I headed north, the Daytona Beach boardwalk passing to the right, wild surf beyond, the tide running high. The winds were up, washing in through the missing passenger side window. Five miles along, it started to rain.

Finding the murder scene was easy.

A sheriff was in the middle of the two-lane, directing traffic, encouraging cars to hurry on by. At his back, a utility truck blocked the southbound lane. A team of workers were busy replacing the fire hydrant that Carson Staines sheared off before running over the man and woman. Yellow crime scene tape marked off thirty yards of shops and sidewalk restaurants.

I parked in front of the beachside restaurant adjoining the pier. Crossing the road, I stood to the side of the fire hydrant and workers. A few yards to my right, the front window of the Flagler Real Estate shop was boarded up. Even after a cleanup and the rain, the sidewalk had rust-colored ghosts of bloodstains.

"Help you?" a deep voice asked.

Beside me was another officer, this one in a jacket, tie, and a sheriff's ball cap.

"I'm trying to understand."

"Aren't we all. Sir, you need to move on." He sounded tired but patient.

"Of course. Up there." I pointed twenty yards farther along the sidewalk. "Is that where he tried to run the kids over?"

His eyes followed mine. A second work crew were replacing the lamp post that had ended Carson Staines' life. The sidewalk was blackened from the fire.

"Do you know something we don't?" His voice perked up.

"No, I don't know anything. Guess I should stop watching television."

"We're you around when this happened?"

"No, I was out of state. Got into Florida last night."

"Where are you from?"

"Michigan, just north of Ann Arbor."

"What brought you down here?"

"Thinking about becoming a snowbird," I lied smoothly, adding, "I'll get out of your way. Sorry to trouble you."

"Sir, what's your name?"

I told him. He asked for my driver's license and copied down its details on a notepad.

"Enjoy Florida." He handed back my license. "My suggestion: turn off your TV and go enjoy the beach. The rains will stop soon."

"Thank you; I will."

After retrieving the Buick, I rolled with the traffic another two blocks into the heart of the idyllic small beach town. Picking out a 7-Eleven just up a way, I turned on the blinkers. While I waited for my chance to turn, I tried to answer the question Buzz Guzman and I had discussed briefly.

"What story did that sad crime scene tell?"

It had to wait until the car was parked and I could use my hands.

Sitting in front of the 7-Eleven, I formed a viewfinder and brought up the details of the sidewalk. Carson Staines had hit the hydrant and the couple at high speed. I saw the path of his car from the corner to where it crashed into the lamppost. He must have been struggling with the wheel after killing the couple and hitting the front of the real estate office. He also hadn't lifted as he raced up the sidewalk. My finger atop the imaginary viewfinder tightened down the focus on the sidewalk before the burn marks from the explosion. Clear as day, there were no skid marks. He was still aiming for his target when the lamppost ended everything. The injured kids were the key.

Lowering the viewfinder, I climbed out and entered the store, gathering copies of the local and state newspapers. I also bought a bottle of water. Minutes later, I sat behind the wheel, searching each paper for news of the *Sidewalk Horror*, as one of them called it. Fifteen minutes later, I knew little more about the kids; their names and statements were not revealed because of their ages. Raindrops were dotting the last newspaper as I closed it. The winds had shifted, and the rains were coming in through the passenger window. Across the parking lot was a dumpster I could lose the papers in.

I climbed out, and there was a worn, oversized beach umbrella opened low in front of the dumpster with three pairs of beat-up sneakers showing. I walked over, saying, "Hello there. Excuse me."

The umbrella tilted back. Three sets of eyes studied me as though trying to determine my intent. They were young kids, looking to be between nine and eleven years old. With my next step closer, they stood as one, the umbrella going back, their expressions hostile and suspicious.

"Just want to toss these." I held up the newspapers.

The boy and girl turned to the girl in the middle. She had a beautiful young face framed in unwashed short black hair. Her chin had a dirt smudge, and her eyes on mine were hard as nails.

"There's a trashcan by the door," she told me.

"You po-lice?" the boy taunted.

"Or a pervo?" the girl on the right jabbed.

"Neither. Just a guy trying to figure out what happened up the street the other day."

"That whack job missed us is what happened." The boy probably said more than he should.

"Shut it," the girl in the middle warned.

"You were there? That car was after you?" I asked, looking face to face for a nod or answer.

"No, not us," The middle girl said.

"Who then?"

"Mister, don't know what you're up to, but piss off," the girl on the right told me.

"In a moment, yes. Can I ask one last question?" All three were poised to run.

"That's it. I'm gone." The girl took off.

"Same. Come, Feeb!" The boy followed her, both running, splashing across the parking lot for the side street.

Only the girl with the umbrella pole on her shoulder remained.

"He's one of our friends," she offered, tight-lipped.

"Right. Can you tell me his name?"

"That's not happening. We're in enough trouble."

"I'm trying to find him and help him," I tried.

"And who are you?"

"My name is Pierce. I believe I'm a relative."

She scoffed, no amusement, saying, "Then you are a liar because all his family is dead."

"Who told you that?"

"He did. Everyone died in Mexico."

That set me back. I looked away. From across the road, waves were booming, exploding on the beach. A montage played without my forming a viewfinder. Kazu on the run in Puerto Mita, believing his family was dead, trying to survive, never once phoning his parents. Why would he?

"Know where he lives?" I asked.

"Lives on the riverside of the island," she answered, adding, "I'm outta here."

The umbrella pole bonked on the pavement before going under her arm.

"Can you give me his address?" I asked.

She was already running.

"Look for the dance house," she called over her shoulder, dashing for the corner of the 7-Eleven and her friends. I watched her until she rounded and disappeared.

"Riverside of the island?" I asked myself. What island?

After shoving the newspapers in the dumpster, I went back inside and bought a local area map. The answer was there before me as I unfolded it. I hadn't known that the Halifax River separated Daytona to Flagler Beach from the mainland.

"The dance house," were her last words. I had no idea what to do with that.

I should have shown her his photograph. I regretted not doing so. It was in my wallet. The image might have won her over. I needed to show it to her if and when I saw her again. Ali had taken the photograph a handful of years before. In it was a younger Kazu with a mischievous smile. He was at the helm of his pirate ship in their swimming pool.

***

The rain let up sometime later. The winds remained as the day turned to late afternoon, a warm, humid day. With the windows missing, the A/C struggled to keep the interior cool as I drove the length of the Halifax River, pulling off onto the grass shoulder often, eyeing the riverfront homes. For the most part, the river was lined with stately homes in the shade of hundred-year-old oak and palm trees. I finished my first trip along the river at the Ponce Inlet waterway to the ocean. I hadn't seen anything that suggested a dance house, whatever that was.

Turning around, I headed north again, looking at each residence, many modern, some from long ago with red-tiled roofs, multiple chimneys, and driveways leading into gardens before double front doors. None of them spoke to me, but I refused to feel discouraged.

Three hours later, I was at the Tomoka Basin, the northern start of the river. There was nothing to do but turn around and start again. I continued until nightfall, looking for anything that suggested "The dance house."

***

Returning to my room at the SeaBreeze, I laid out dinner from a greasy paper bag and kicked off my shoes.

I let the doubts and questions come on in. The girl at the 7-Eleven, the one her friends called Feeb, could have easily lied to send me off down a rabbit trail, just to get rid of me. I can't say I blamed her. Some *adult* asking questions when she and the other two were already in trouble, as they had said.

My thoughts turned to the question of *him*. I had to take a stand.

He was no longer Jappy, that offensive slur. Yes, his father was Japanese; but that didn't excuse the nickname. From now on, he wasn't the boy, either.

He was Kazu.

Kazu Danser.

And he would be until I was proved wrong.

That decided, I ate my Christmas dinner, showered, and went to bed.

Chapter Sixteen

"The dance house"

I woke to a text message alert, my iPhone hidden in the bedding. Digging out the buzzing device, I held it up before my sleepy eyes. The Los Angeles area code was familiar; the rest of the number was new. I opened the message.

> Pie. Turn. And run.
> You've poked your wanger in the wrong hole.
> You have to step back, step away.
> They know where your son and family live.
> And, Pie, I've confirmed that the boy isn't Kazu.
> Rhonda

"Run?" From Rhonda?

I dialed her number. A young woman answered, "Blue Wave Studios, this is Candice Wales: how may I assist you?"

"Hello, Candice. Where's Rhonda?"

"Who's calling, please?"

"Pierce Danser. Where is she? Why are you answering her line?"

"Oh," was followed by, "one moment, please."

Her *moment* was two minutes long as I sat on hold, listening to the studio's choice of music: baroque and dramatic.

"Pierce? Let me call you back on my cell," Candice returned to the call.

She hung up, and my cell lit up thirty seconds later.

"Pierce, it's Candice. She disappeared. Studio security is buzzing. I'm really scared for her."

"Have they brought in the police?" I asked.

"If they have, they aren't saying. I was told to go back to work."

"Where do they think she is?"

"They're not answering questions. Only asking them."

The Hollywood way. Everything stays inside the studio's hive.

"When was she last seen?"

"Yesterday morning. We were both in the office, enjoying the holiday quiet to get some work done. Just after nine, she said she was going down to her car for some files. Never returned. Left without her purse and worse, without her phone."

Where was the minder we had hired to watch over her? That was my next call. I thanked Candice, asked her to call me with any news, and rang off.

Dialing 0, I had the operator connect me. Three minutes later, after being placed on hold and transferred twice, I had Lance Jones on the line. He was expecting my call, answering with, "Hello, Mr. Danser, we're on it."

"Where was your guy?"

"Distracted briefly. Now unemployed."

"Have you called in the police?"

"We had hoped not to, but yes. Have a meeting with them in a few minutes."

"She texted me."

"When?"

"A half-hour ago."

"Read it back to me, please."

I did.

"That helps."

"How's that?"

"She's worried about you and whatever 'Kazu' is about and not her situation."

It was a good point. The problem with text messages was the lack of voice or tone.

"Her parents okay?" I asked.

"Yes," Lance answered, sounding more confident. "We've doubled up on them."

"What can I do?"

"Leave this to us. I'll keep you posted. Take Rhonda's advice."

Take Rhonda's advice?

How could I? This was my grandson we were searching for.

How could I not if continuing meant Rhoda and my family were threatened?

"Thank you," I ended the call, deciding that I needed to lighten my step but not turn around.

I showered, pulled on clean clothes, and left the motel. The temperature was in the seventies, with rain and gusts of winds. On the sidewalks along the beachside hotels and condo towers, vacationers walked in packs, drenched and grinning. Enjoying their warm retreat from the northern frozen cities, likely thinking, "Florida? This all you got for winter?" I turned west, away from the coast.

For the next two hours, I played lost and confused tourist driving along the Halifax River, planning to say I was home shopping if stopped or questioned by anyone. It was about as light-footed as I knew how to be.

Buzz Guzman called me at ten that morning.

"Good progress on the laptop. They have the drive back to life and are working on data transfer and repairs."

"How long?"

"Tonight. Tomorrow morning at the worst."

"Good. Thank you. And?"

"Our friend Rex from Texas. He's working for someone who works for someone who wants you stopped. It's not confirmed, but he's surely got the contract on the boy."

"Damn. Buzz, I had a scary text from Rhonda—"

"She's the woman you told me was helping you out before?"

"Yes. She asked me to stop the hunt. It gets worse. She's disappeared."

We were both silent with that. I pulled off onto the shoulder and parked on the grass between two large riverfront homes.

"Okay, here's what we do," Buzz said. "We submerge but continue. Are the police searching for Rhonda?"

"Yes. And a private investigator I hired."

"Okay… Good. So, we don't do anything to rattle them. There's plenty we can do. The laptop for one. Did you send her a reply?"

"No."

"Do so. Tell her you're backing off, no, that you've stopped searching. Say you're convinced it's all been foolish. That it isn't him."

"Okay. I'll send it after we hang up."

"Good. Could help get her released."

"I should have thought of that."

"It's my job to think this way, not yours."

I told him about Feeb, the girl from the 7-Eleven, and my search for 'the dance house' on the riverside of the island.

"Continue that," Buzz said. "My next stop is in Ponce Inlet. See what the techie has on the reporter's laptop. Let's meet up this evening."

We ended the call and I continued my house to house, looking for anything that suggested "dance."

An hour passed. None of the impressive homes, old or new, spoke to me. Another hour went by. I was frustrated and worse, letting doubt creep in. When I reached the Tomoka Basin to the north, I stopped instead of turning around for another lap.

"This ain't working," I decided. Plan B came quickly. Find that girl, Feeb, and persuade her to give me more details on Kazu's location.

I drove along the Halifax River, looking for a road running to the coast. Once I reached A1A, finding the 7-Eleven would be easy.

Turning on Sea Vista Drive, I hoped it ran to the beachside. As if on cue, the clouds rolled back, and I was bathed in fine Florida sunshine. The details crisp, the ripe colors of the world returned. An hour or so of this heat would dry out the interior of the car. Nothing to do about the front seats still salt and peppered with broken glass. Sea Vista Drive resembled a spilled Easter basket, each home a warm pastel of apricot, cool blue, and creamy orange, among other colors. The road ended abruptly at a stop sign before A1A, which was filled with racing holiday traffic.

I came to a stop, turned the left blinkers on and never saw it coming. The impact drove my head forward, clouting the steering wheel. In the rearview mirror was a white and orange U-Haul van. The impact had shoved the Buick ten feet forward, almost into the oncoming traffic.

Thinking it was insurance card and driver's license exchange time, I put the car in park and dug for my wallet. That's when the U-Haul struck again: crunching and rending metal and something else; the van's racing engine and spinning tires.

The driver was hard on the accelerator, my car skidding, sliding out into the streaming traffic on A1A.

To my left was an oncoming RV, fifteen tons of metal running fast, doing at least seventy miles per hour. I slammed my foot on the brake for all the good that did. The Buick was raised at the rear and still being shoved out onto the highway.

In seconds, I would be out in front of that approaching RV and the stream of cars following it. I dropped the column arm into drive. I didn't know what else to do, but sometimes you have to get off the brake and mash your foot on the throttle.

How the RV and the trailing cars missed, I'll leave to my lucky stars.

The Buick raced across the highway and into a six-foot berm of dense palmetto. Horns and brakes were screaming behind me. I had my hands full, still hunched for an expected impact. The car crunched against hidden stones as I spun the wheel, struggling to avoid going over the rise.

I got the car turned before it crashed down the cliff to the beach below. The Buick was rolling and striking rocks, raised on its right side. I bounced and bucked that way, steering for a turnout twenty yards away.

When I stopped the Buick, the U-Haul was gone, like it had never been there. I looked up and down A1A before accepting it must have run off back up Sea Vista.

"Who?"

I had a guess.

"Why?"

Like Rhonda had said, to turn me away.

I climbed out, my head splitting from a new form of headache rising through my neck. Traffic was running hot both north and south, washing the turnout with hot wind.

Circling, I saw the two right-side tires flat and sagging in the white sand. I checked out the rear of the car. The bumper was somewhere but no longer attached to the Buick. The taillights were shattered and the trunk lid was mashed and raised.

I found my phone on the passenger floorboard and figured out how to search for "tow trucks." While waiting for it to arrive, I watched the streaming traffic for any hint of the white and orange van—no idea if he was coming back for another strike.

My face aching, my bloody nose dotting my shirt, I ignored both and the headache as best I could. Time for licking my wounds had to wait until I was somewhere safe.

I remained vigilant, ready to jump off the edge of the turnout and down onto the beach if needed. Studying the traffic coming in both directions, I dialed 9-1-1 and reported the accident, and no, I didn't have the van's license plate number.

The tow truck arrived a half-hour later. If the police were headed out to write up the accident, I didn't know. After loading up the battered Buick, the driver took me south into Ormond Beach to A1A Auto Repair, sharing the building with the post office.

While the car was unloaded, I went inside, entering a time capsule circa 1940s. The office was dark and a riot of clutter. The sturdy, child-sized front desk was stacked with auto parts and grease-marked stacks of paperwork. Behind it sat a short man, unshaven, with a boxer's face.

"Hello, I'll need a couple of new tires," I explained.

"What did you hit?"

"Rocks and weeds."

"We'll gladly look at it. Please, take a seat in the waiting room."

He apparently didn't need me to fill out any paperwork. As he headed out into the garage through a side door, I wandered in through a doorway to the right, assuming it was the waiting room. There were three plastic chairs, a scatter of old auto magazines on side tables, two televisions playing from the top of filing cabinets. The space smelled of burnt coffee and the dust of decades.

I wasn't alone. A man about my age was sitting in the third orange chair, boot extended. He looked like what I supposed a Florida farmer would: worn blue jeans, black and brown Pendleton shirt, a John Deere baseball cap. His face was tanned and wrinkled.

"Hey there," he offered, not looking my way, his eyes glued to the two televisions. He was grinning, and as I sat, I watched him start to whisper and smile. I looked to see what was amusing him.

Both televisions were muted. One showed a soap opera.

The other was on a sports channel. He was talking to the one showing a silver-haired man in formal wear standing before a prim, wealthy woman and a beautiful young girl.

The farmer snickered, paused, and whispered again. I had to ask.

"Whatcha doing?"

"Overdubbing the dialogue. Ever do that?"

Before I could say I hadn't, he added, "TV can be okay when ya play with it."

I nodded.

"Those three," he pointed to the soap opera being played out in a modern business office.

"Wait," he whispered a line of dialogue and gave a hearty chuckle. Shaking his head, he explained, "I have the three of them discussing their joys of sodomy and preferences for lubricant and sex toys."

Looking at the three formally attired, serious actors on the screen, I had to admit his take on them was funny. Much more amusing than whatever drama they were struggling through if the sound was up.

"But darling, KY is a family tradition," he had the prime, pouting woman say.

I laughed. It felt good. It had been a while.

The farmer pointed to the second television, "Those two… any guess?"

"Not a one," I smiled, looking at the excited talking heads of former athletes ranting across a studio desk of microphones and coffee cups.

"Last hour, they were nothing but the barks and calls of monkeys. That got old cause I couldn't improvise much with those, so now they're scared witless, all red-faced over the unstoppable zombie invasion."

I liked it. It made as much sense as anything appearing on television, and he was right. Why sit and blandly watch when you could instead interact and have some laughs? I reclined, and for the next half-hour, I enjoyed his adlibbing.

When the shop owner leaned in through the door, he said to me, "Tires done. Put on a couple of fresh retreads. Saved you a few bucks."

"Thank you." I stood to follow him to the office.

"Take care," I offered the farmer, but he was engrossed with the two comical dramas.

"Not tryin' to upsell you," the shop man said, "but you should let us check the right-side steering. It's banged up good." He circled the deck to his battered office chair.

"How bad is it? I'm in a bit of a hurry."

"It'll be drivable, but not for long."

"I'll stop back in as soon as things settle down," I lied. "How much do I owe you?"

The price was ridiculously low. There still wasn't a need for any paperwork. A handshake settled us up after he ran my credit card.

Keys in hand, I walked out to the sad and battered-looking Buick. I had two fresh right-side tires, no hubcaps. The trunk lid was permanently open, the front windows gone, the right side dented and scraped from the wild bashing an hour or so before.

Climbing in behind the wheel, my short respite was over. Starting the engine, I was one hundred percent back in the frightening world of the hunt. Turning out onto northbound A1A, I was focused and determined. The auto shop owner was true to his word. As I accelerated up the highway for Flagler Beach, the steering felt loose and had a constant pull to the right.

***

Returning to the 7-Eleven, I pulled to the right of the glass doors. There was a group of five kids with skateboards hanging out in front of the dumpster. All five were dressed in faded, threadbare shorts and shirts, their hair dirty, their grins to one another secretive. I walked over slowly, casually, smiling, trying not to look like a threat. My smile was stared down with each step closer.

I didn't see the girl, Feeb, among them but remembered one of the boy's faces from the day before. He set his Slurpee on the pavement and stepped in front of the others.

"This man was bugging Feeb yesterday," he said, not turning around.

"Just some questions, nothing else." I was still smiling, hoping they wouldn't run.

I got out my wallet and opened it. Five pairs of distrusting eyes watched my hands. The blonde girl to the right, the tallest, stepped forward. She tiptoed and peered inside.

"What's your name?" I asked her.

"Bikes. You gonna like bribe us?"

"I hadn't thought of that, but sure." I took out the old photograph of Kazu instead of cash.

She took the photograph in her small, dirty hands and smiled in recognition, I was sure.

"I'm trying to find him is all." I watched her hand the photograph to the boy.

"What do you want with him?"

"I'd like to help him get home."

"He ain't got no home. You're lying. His family is dead."

He pressed the photograph back to me. "What do you really want?"

I wasn't going to argue about the misunderstanding. "I simply want to talk with him. I'm not a policeman; nothing like that. Yesterday, Feeb helped me locate where he's hiding. I only want to ask her for a few more details."

"She ain't here. What kind of details?" Bikes, the girl, asked.

"A street number for a dance house."

"Ain't one," the boy chimed in.

"You know where he is?" I asked.

"Never went there," Bikes said, "it was his secret."

"I did," the boy said. "One time. Helped him hide stolen bikes there."

"Can it, Slurp," Bikes scolded.

"Okay, no street number," I said. "Remember what color the house was?"

"Sort of," the boy said.

"Sort of?" I pressed as gently as I could.

"Old."

"Dude, old isn't a color." Bikes shook her head.

He ignored her. "It's like a jungle along the back… with high walls."

"Anything else you remember?" I asked.

"Place had a wicked vibe and a long dock."

"Would you be willing to come along and show me?"

He leaned to the side and eyed the battered Buick.

"No way. That's a serious creep car."

"Buy us a round of Slurpee's, mister?" Bikes was clearly done with the topic of Kazu and his mysterious hiding place.

"Sure," I said. They had given me additional information.

We all went inside and while they poured themselves jumbo Slurpees, I found a coil of white quarter-inch twine, the strongest they had. The five kids took off as I paid the cashier.

When I went back outside, I was greeted by rain and lightning and thunder like artillery in the movies. The storm rolled in, just like that. I guessed it was a Florida thing.

Around the corner of the store appeared the girl, Feeb, under her large beach umbrella. She wore black high-top sneakers and a black smock dress.

When she saw me, she collapsed the umbrella, smiled, and in a flash, turned and ran.

The other kids were laughing as she dashed around the building front and disappeared.

"Never catch her," Bikes laughed the loudest.

***

After tying down the flapping trunk lid, I drove south and took the first road to the right that looked like it would run to the Halifax River. All I had to find was a jungle house with stone walls and a wicked long dock. It should be easy, right?

I continued my house-to-house search beyond the Tomoka Basin that fed the Halifax, driving slowly, the wipers sweeping off the rain. It would be dark within the hour, making the search more difficult.

There were quite a few residences with wicked long docks, overgrown plants and vegetation and stone walls. I parked and approached three, Kazu's photograph in hand, hoping that would get the homeowner talking. It didn't take long to figure out that the homes were vacant—the dropped storm shutters saying, "We also live elsewhere."

The night wore on. I guesstimated that I was about halfway along the way to Ponce Inlet, checking out the homes. Drawing close to one of the arched bridges that crossed the wide river for the mainland, I pulled over. Daylight would make this so much easier.

To my right was what I guessed was a boathouse out on the water. It was tall and squat, and as best I could see, it had no door or windows or a walkway to it. There was also a long empty dock to the left.

On the other side of the road was a high wall of pale stone, ten feet tall with clinging ivy. The wall was nearly a block long.

"A private park? A cemetery?" I wondered.

At its center was a faint glowing bulb. Looking along the wall again, mildly curious about what it contained, I climbed out. It was iffy at best, but it felt good to stretch my legs. I crossed the road and entered the vegetation, there being no walkway. I saw that the red bulb was atop a metal box against the wall and trudged through overgrown weeds and palmetto to it. By then,

I could make out a heavy-looking wood door, half-hidden by dangling vines.

A rust-mottled button centered the metal box. When I pushed it, the red bulb turned green, and I heard gears turning a camera somewhere above. There was an electronic screech, followed twenty seconds later by a woman's sleepy voice.

"Aunt Izzy, who you be?"

"Pierce Danser, looking for a boy, named—"

"You damned drunk. Waking me for this? Bugger off."

The camera clicked. The bulb on the box returned to red.

I stepped back, still wondering about what the wall contained.

"A compound?" I asked. "With what? An eccentric recluse?"

It made as much sense as anything. I turned away. I was tired. This was a waste of time. I had to pee. My phone purred.

"Pierce, it's Buzz. Got some good news."

"Need it. I'm out waking old ladies for no good reason."

"I won't ask. The laptop is cracked. I just sent you a series of documents and a second photo."

"Sent it how?" Did he have my hotel fax number? I don't think I'd ever mentioned I was staying at the Sea Breeze motel.

"Your phone, you luddite," he laughed.

My "oh…" added to his merriment.

I lowered the phone from my ear, casting my chest in its light. I would need more than a few minutes to figure out how to look at documents and the second photo, but I would not ask for help unless I had to.

"Gimme a second," I lied.

A glint of brass caught my eye, the phone's light reflecting on it. It was coming from the side of the heavy wood door. I reached out to brush the ivy aside.

"Got them?" Buzz asked. "The third document has all the reporter's last notes before he went nuts in his car."

"Almost," I lied again. Turning the phone to use as a light, I lifted the ivy from the inscription on a brass plate embedded in the pale stone. I read it. And reread it.

"Buzz, let me call you back," I said absently, the files and photograph needed to wait a few. The etched plate was surely a hundred or more years old.

What it said to me was, "Come back here at first light."

It read:

Maison de Danse

Chapter Seventeen

Maison de Danse

Back inside the Sea Breeze motel room, I set my drive-thru dinner in a greasy white bag on the nightstand and sat on the bed, phone in hand. There was a single message from Lance, the security detective in Los Angeles.

"Hello, Mr. Danser, a brief status report. Good progress, but a ways to go. The police have assigned an investigator from the missing bureau while I work the back streets for chatter. First, if you didn't hear, Rhonda's car never left the studio lot. Second, it's not a boyfriend or lover or favorite hump—excuse that. Her folks are safe and, of course, in a tizzy about their daughter. My money is on this not being some whack job. This was too organized, more like a snatch for cash. My next task? Find out who has her and once I know that, negotiate a swap. We're likely dealing with a cholo gang. I'll know soon. Any swap will certainly be an expensive one so that you're prepared. I'll call you tomorrow midday. We'll find her."

That was *almost* reassuring. I felt terrible about getting Rhonda entangled. I felt worse for not being able to do anything more than write checks.

Closing the voicemail, I figured out how to retrieve and open the files that Buzz Guzman had sent. There were two lengthy documents and a single photograph attached. I passed on Carson Staines' writings and opened the photograph.

The image was taken from an airport security camera, from the side and above. The image was in color. Unfortunately, the boy's face was blocked by his hat.

And that was the answer, the confirmation. At last, I was sure: the full golden Pittsburg Pirates "P" on the black baseball cap was as clear as day.

Getting up from the side of the bed, I started the shower and stripped off my clothes. Under the streaming warm water, I formed a viewfinder with my thumbs and fingers. A new collage began to reveal itself. This one had a theme, a gift from the photograph on my phone.

Kazu on the beach, walking along the waterline. Eyes relaxed, not worried or scared; no over-the-shoulder glances. His family was in the frame, in the foreground—the camera was above and looking over their shoulders. Bill, Ali, and Dan the Baby had spotted Kazu, and their fears and pains were receding.

Kazu hadn't spotted them yet. He was walking with his eyes to the waves breaking along the shore, his lips showing in the shadow of his baseball cap.

Bill called out to him.

Kazu turned. And there were his eyes, showing relief and delight and surprise. His past years of terrifying survival were over.

He saw his parents and baby brother alive and well and ran across the sand to them, arms open wide.

***

At six the following day, I woke up sharing the bed with the paper wrappers from dinner the night before. My plan was to head back to the gate door of the Maison de Danse residence and persuade that Aunt Izzy to talk to me. Seeing no new messages on the phone, I headed out.

The beat-up rental was parked nose-in, a few steps from my front door. The fog had rolled in from the ocean, and the car was beaded with sea mist. Unlocking the door, I saw a folded note set under the wiper blade. Getting in behind the wheel, I unfolded the two-squared piece of soggy paper. It was a crude drawing, like something done by a child, a top-down sketch of what looked like a street with a square in the middle. There was a red scribbled circle on the right side of the square.

My phone rang. No number displayed.

"Go there. I need to talk to you," a gruff male voice ordered, no nonsense, followed by the end-of-call tone.

I saw two words written across the bottom: "Daytona Pier."

Turning on the seat, I scanned three hundred sixty degrees. I knew from the timing of the call that I was being watched. There was nothing but an early, foggy motel parking lot and the row of rooms facing it.

I called Buzz to ask how best to handle this. Hitting voicemail, I said, "That Rex from Texas called. I'm going to go meet him."

Climbing out, I went inside the motel office and got one of those colorful tourist maps. Locating the Daytona beach Pier was easy.

After parking in a sandlot back of the boardwalk, I walked the gift shops and fried-everything walk-up restaurants to the concrete stairs leading out into the pier. The square on the map that Rex had put on my windshield was the modern, two-story Joe's Crab Shack in the middle of the pier. The sky was gray, the wind cold. The place looked closed and only a few people were milling about, braving the chill.

I took a table where the red circle was on the map, choosing the chair in the outdoor dining area facing the restaurant. Wishing there was a wall at my back, I had to do with the railing above the eighty-foot drop to the water.

A man came out through the restaurant doors, surprising me. I thought the place was closed for the morning. Dressed all in black, my first thought was, "A waiter," except he wasn't carrying menus, and his eyes were those of a viper aimed at me. He was a thin man with blond highlighted hair and a goat tuff under his lower lip. He had pasty white skin and deadly blue eyes, a handsome man in serious need of some sun. He smiled at me, the expression not changing his hard gaze.

He sat beside me instead of across, making me uncomfortable as I bet he expected.

"Thank you," were his first words.

"For?"

"Ya led us to him."

"Us?"

"Dang, ain't that a slip. There's no us, just my employer and me." Unlike his earlier voice on the phone, here was a full-blown Texan twang.

"They want him because they think he stole some money?" I asked.

"Not my concern, but I've heard he also shot the wrong guy."

I looked away; we were very much alone on the outdoor deck. Nothing but a few seagulls looking dull and hopeful.

"Why did you want to talk to me?" I asked.

"Ever notice that in Disney films, the only good moms are the dead moms. I see you in the mom role for the boy," he paused and looked to the restaurant doors, adding, "good help's hard to find."

"It's too early," I said like it mattered.

"So, let me tell you how this whole rodeo's gonna play out," he continued. "One. You walk away. Go home. Sell cars. Two. I get the boy. Turn him over."

I hadn't heard or noticed the waiter approach, even facing the doors. I was studying Rex's pale and confident expression. Two tall drinks were placed on the table.

"Anything else, gentlemen?" the waiter asked. Neither Rex nor I replied, and he left us alone.

"Persuaded the manager to open early. Just for you and I," Rex said. He clicked the bottom of his glass against the top of mine.

"You were once a drunkard, right?" He raised his glass and took two healthy gulps. "Seen a lot of that. Understand kicking it is like sex with a gorilla. You don't stop until the gorilla wants to."

I had heard that one before and stared at his face, hidden by the raised bottom of his drink.

"I don't drink. Alcohol is for the amateurs at life," I dug at him, watching him swallow.

"Whatever you mean by that. Here's what's happenin' next. You climb into your piece of shit rental and skedaddle north to where you belong."

"And?" I asked, trying my best to ignore the drink very close to my hand, studying his distant blue eyes.

"All I'm gonna do is get him to a safe room and secure him and hand him the phone. After he's told them where the money is, they'll be done with him."

"And then you let him go?" I said, my voice sarcastic. I shook my head at his absurd lie.

"Best deal ya got. I can at least keep him in the States and outta their hands."

I decided to go along with this fantasy, asking, "You don't plan to harm him?"

"As soon as the boy's sung his song, I'll let you know. I'll even pay for his flight. Wherever you like." Rex turned and waved to the waiter by the door, calling out, "Two more double Tanqueray's."

He had finished his first. I had stopped glancing at mine.

"How much?" I asked.

"For?"

I pushed my drink toward him across the table. "For *you* to walk away."

He laughed—a gravelly sputter. Scooting his chair back, he unzipped his windbreaker.

The second round of drinks was set on the table. Rex turned and watched the waiter until he went inside.

He opened the left side of his jacket, revealing the gun holster at his side. The leather looked worked and weathered, which said something. Reaching across himself with his right hand, he drew out the handgun with a silencer on the barrel.

"Some tourist disappears. Happens a lot."

I watched the gun as it turned from me.

"Wanna see how easy?"

Three feet away, two seagulls were up on the view rail, beggars with wings.

The gun spit, barely cracking the air.

The bird on the left exploded in a spray of feathers and blood, the remains launched and falling to the waves below the pier.

"I'm not for sale," he said. "Already hired out."

Rex laid another card on the table, so to speak.

"Your old partner, Rhonda, the girl in L.A., is going to remain on ice until you leave all this. If you don't take my advice? Maybe some gator hole for you. You're here all alone, easy to disappear."

The gruesome threat set me back in my chair. But his words said something else. He didn't know about Buzz Guzman, one of my few cards.

Holstering the gun, Rex said, "So what are you going to do?"

Instead of answering that, I said, "Received a photograph of the boy this morning. It's not my grandson." I hoped the lie sounded sad.

Rex studied my face, his expression blank. If that information affected him, he wasn't showing.

"So, yes, I'm headed home today," I told him.

"I'm supposed to believe that?"

"Yes, you are."

I looked at the two morning cocktails before me, seductive as always. Picking up the drink before me, I poured it out on the restaurant deck. Did the same with the second and stood to leave.

"I have no reason to stick around. Hate what's happening to that kid, but I've got a grandson to try to find."

My phone rang. I ignored it. I started walking away, not at all comfortable with Rex and his gun at my back. Out on the pier, instead of checking to see who had just called, I dialed

Buck's Gun Rack and asked, "What time do you open tomorrow morning?"

My three-day cool-off period would be over.

***

Back at the Sea Breeze motel, I packed my suitcase and files and left. I would need to find a new motel that night to hide from Rex from Texas. Pulling out onto A1A, I played Buzz Guzman's voicemail.

"I would have come, but you didn't tell me where you were meeting him. Call me if you get this before you head out. Hell, call me either way."

Wishing I had done so, I drove north, crossing East Granada, which led to the bridge from the island. Taking the next road to the right, I went west until I reached the riverfront road.

A half-mile from the wall of the Maison de Danse, I dialed Buzz's number. Cursed voicemail.

"Hey, Buzz, it's Pierce. It *is* my grandson. Thank you for sending me the photograph..."

The phone rang. I didn't know it could receive calls while leaving a message. I tapped the button to take the call.

"Did you read Carson Staines' files?" Buzz asked.

"No, but I will."

"You need to. When and where do you meet with our Rex Thurges?"

"Already did. A dangerous guy. With a gun. He told me to walk away… or he'd shoot me like a seagull."

"Whatever that means. What did you tell him?"

"That I was leaving. That the latest photograph proved the boy isn't Kazu."

"Good. No more meetings with Rex from Texas without me, got that?"

"Yes," I agreed.

"What did he want?"

"To scare the hell out me, which he did. Convince me to walk away. He also said his partners or whatever they are have Rhonda and will release her once I leave."

There was silence. I hoped Buzz was coming up with a brilliant new plan.

"Read the files," he said. "Let's meet for lunch. The same Waffle House. I've got a bead on Rex from Texas," he went on. "More than a bead, some good leverage. I'll explain when we meet."

"I will after I check out a place."

"What place?"

"A big house. Some kids suggested it's where Kazu lives."

"Some kids told you that, and you're running with it?" I could hear the skepticism loud and clear.

"They're his friends."

"Well, good luck with that. Let me know how it goes. See you at noon."

With the call over, I drove the rest of the way along the Halifax River to the front of the long wall with its gate and camera.

Seeing the place in daylight helped some. I saw the wall was indeed a block long. It had been built with pale sand-colored stone, most of it hidden by climbing ivy. Large oaks with Spanish moss showed beyond the top of the wall.

Before climbing out, I dialed Lance the investigator, to see where he was with finding Rhonda.

Does anyone answer their calls anymore? True, there were time differences between the east and west coast, so it was three hours earlier out there. I left a message asking for a status.

Walking up through the grass and ivy, I heard a distant piano playing from somewhere beyond that tall wall. I rang the bell like the night before and waited, offering a smile I didn't feel to the camera whirring above.

After a minute, I pushed the button again.

The music ended, and I stood in silence.

Wondering if I could climb the ten-foot wall, I looked for hand and footholds.

At the right side of the gate, I tested vines until I found one I thought might take my weight. Climbing within a foot of the top of the wall, I heard the familiar squeal of electricity from the box beside the gate. I boosted myself up and got a quick glimpse of the other side.

This was much more than a residence, the Maison de Danse resembled a family compound, looking like it might possibly reach all the way east to the ocean. One end on the beach and the other on the river? It was an old place overgrown with vegetation, at least from what I saw briefly.

Letting go, I fell and stepped over to the box beside the gate. A familiar electronic squelch came from the box beside the gate.

"You're back. Why?" the same woman from the previous night asked.

Good question. *Because some kids told me*… I shook my head, saying a single word.

"Kazu."

"Ka-zu? And what is that? Like the noisemaker?"

"It's a boy's name. My grandson's name."

"Who in the hell names a boy that?"

I paused. We were off on the wrong foot. "You're Aunt Izzy,

right?"

"Yes. I'm Aunt Izzy, but not your Aunt Izzy."

"Right, got that straight. Any chance you've got a twelve-year-old boy staying with you?"

I got my first taste of Aunt Izzy's laughter, rich in sarcasm and dismissal. "No kept men, no kept boys, either. Go away."

"By the way, what is this place?" I tried, hoping to keep her talking. "It's huge and impressive."

"Goodbye, whoever you are. Don'tcha come back, or I'll have the po-lice all over you." And with that, she killed the conversation.

Frustrated, I stared at the gate, hoping to hear the lock click, wishing her a change of heart. Three minutes later, I was back behind the wheel of the Buick.

A U-Haul van rolled by. I didn't see its front end, so I couldn't say if it was bashed in or not. This was a coincidence I wasn't comfortable with, not with Rex from Texas and his silenced handgun. Knowing I would arrive early, I headed over to the Waffle House in Daytona Beach. Having a faint idea about how to lose Rex from Texas, I planned to use the time to think it through.

After scanning the mirrors while circling the Waffle House, I parked the Buick behind the diner. I carried my briefcase inside and took a table near the back.

The next forty minutes were spent with my phone, skim reading the files from Carson Staines' laptop. There were his news articles in draft form before he sent them to the newspapers. Nothing I hadn't already read. Using the date stamps on the files, I scanned his last private words and entered the world of his spiral away from sanity.

The dead reporter had turned up the fires of his hatred of Jappy, devolving into disjointed paragraphs. Adding fuel to the fire, he ranted about vengeance and putting down rabid dogs, his last page a bulleted list of accusations against Jappy.

The final line was, "GONNA SPLAT THE JAP."

Closing the document, I opened my briefcase at my side and I took out the USA map purchased days before. It looked like about twelve hundred miles to my Michigan home. What was that, two days or a through-the-night blast with coffee and gas stops?

Buzz Guzman sat down across from me.

"Planning a road trip?" He nodded to the map in my hands.

"Doubt I can shake him, but I think I can mislead him."

I told Buzz my plan.

"Not a bad idea," he replied when I was done. "I can handle things here. Also, going

to nail down where that scumbag is staying."

"Thank you. Call me if you need anything or if there's any news."

We ordered lunch and ate quickly, talking little. Ten minutes later, I was on the road.

I drove along South Atlantic for Flagler Beach. Entering Ormond by the Sea, the U-Haul van picked me up and stayed three cars back as we drove along the endless beaches and surf. Turning west on Moody Boulevard, I went up and over the long arcing bridge from the island and continued until I came to the ramp for northbound Highway 95.

The Buick was a handful when up to full speed with its damaged front suspension, the steering pulling to the left. A half-hour along, I figured out how to keep the car running straight and true. I had seen the U-Haul van follow me up the on-ramp and saw it again a few miles further, laying back but still trailing.

"Follow me all the way," I told the rearview mirror. Every minute behind me kept Rex from Texas off Kazu's tail and let Buzz do his magic and find him.

I crossed into Georgia some hours later. The miles began to hypnotize me, which was welcomed. I got to Savannah before needing to refuel and did so, watching the off-ramp for the white and orange van. Not spotting it, but sure it was still on me, I jumped back on Highway 95 and continued my northern run.

Night fell. By then, I was in South Carolina. Outside of Florence, I picked out the sign for a Days Inn and switched on the blinkers. After picking up a drive-through diner, I prepaid fifty-four dollars for a room.

I was tired. Sleep was calling me to the bed. I thought putting together a viewfinder would help but chose not to. What would it show me besides a row of question marks about what I was doing?

Pulling on a fresh shirt and pants, I went back out into the night. Under the pretense of retrieving my briefcase, I scanned the parking lot and side streets for the U-Haul van. Not seeing it, I went back inside my room. Sitting on the bed with the unopened briefcase, I closed my eyes, needing the rest, but not laying back. An hour later, I went for a walk in the warm southern night. Taking my time, I walked the streets and parking lots, searching for the U-Haul. I did two rounds of the area, seeing no sign of it.

As planned, ten minutes later, I was back behind the wheel, headed south.

Chapter Eighteen

Rex from Texas

I woke in the back seat of the Buick, parked in a sandlot along the ocean in Ormond Beach, Florida. I could have slept longer, as uncomfortable as it was, but the rain was spitting in through the missing front windows. Climbing out, I stretched and bent and climbed in behind the wheel.

The sunrise was gray and warm, with rain falling and no winds. Buck's Gun Rack opened at 10 a.m. I cooled my jets out front until the many locks were opened and the lights were turned on.

The man behind the glass case of handguns and accessories remembered me from three days before. It took no more than ten minutes and a couple of signatures before I left with the Glock 9mm in hand.

Growing more confident with using my phone for driving directions, I found my way to the Strickland Shooting Range out on Indian Lake Road. I bought a day pass for ten dollars and carried the Glock and the box of hollow tips to what looked like a row of voting booths with tables. I chose the enclosure with the closest target: ten yards away.

It took me forever to load my first clip. It's not easy work pressing one bullet after another inside with the strong string pushing back hard. The model of Glock I had purchased held ten rounds. Putting on the loaner headphones, I struggled to find and release the safety before going with three round bursts, having heard somewhere that that was the best way. I was terrible but improved, hitting the sides of the target three times with the first clip.

The woman in the next booth was deadly earnest, quick and accurate. She worked from a row of spare clips on her table. I watched her and tried to learn while fumbling to load another ten bullets, the air filled with the smell of burnt metal and gunfire from both of my sides.

I emptied the gun at the target, getting four out of ten, reloaded, and got the same results with the next clip. Reloading, I felt my phone ring, doing its buzzing dance in my pocket. I put the Glock on safety and took it out, the gun and clip on the table.

"Where are you?" Buzz Guzman asked. "I hear gunfire."

"Firing range. I'm dreadful but improving. Sort of."

Someone two booths down pulled the trigger on an absurdly loud automatic rifle. I've no idea what Buzz said during that.

"Let me call you back," I told him as the din settled. "It's loud here."

After loading the clip, I pushed it home inside the gun and left, calling him back when I was inside the Buick.

"I think it best you come and get me," Buzz answered. "Did you get a conceal and carry?"

My pause answered that.

"Doubt you're going to need the gun for this. I'm staying at the Daytona Hilton. You can drive and I'll keep an eye on things."

"Where are we going? I think I should get a different car. He's going to recognize this thing soon."

"Good idea, but that can wait. Learned where he's staying. He won't see us coming."

Knowing that the ruined rental car was a red flag, all I had was hope that it wouldn't be spotted. I took back streets until I was in Daytona. There was no sign of the white and orange U-Haul van with a smashed grill. On the way east to South Atlantic, I called Lance, the private detective, for the latest on his hunt for Rhonda. I hit voicemail and left a message asking for a status.

Buzz was waiting out front of the towering hotel, off to the side of the valet podium. He climbed in, saying, "Go west and turn left on North Halifax."

"What are we doing?" I asked.

"He's got himself a loaner condo on the river. The Riverside, unit 2N. That says second floor to me."

"And?"

"You're going to stay in the car while I work some *persuasion*. It goes bad, you're the getaway driver. But that ain't happening."

"Buzz? I tried that when he and I talked on the pier."

"Yes. *Before* you ran back home to Michigan. All I'm doing now is offering to help him hunt down the kid. Convince him I have resources he doesn't."

"You'd know better than I, but he didn't strike me as the kind who plays well with others. Had that whole lone wolf thing going when we met."

"When I bought his location, I heard an odd story. There are possibly two hunters hired for the job. He's got competition, and I'm sure that if he fails, he gets paid nothing."

"Any idea who?"

"No idea if it's even true. A common tactic. If one fails, the backup rides in. I'm trying to chase the rumor down. Turn here."

I turned onto North Halifax, and we drove along the river.

My phone buzzed on the dashboard.

"Look at that," I said, showing the phone to Buzz.

"Whose number is blocked?" he asked.

"Know of only one. It's him."

"Put it on speaker."

I pulled over on the side of the road and did so.

"You should get yourself a new ride," Rex from Texas said. "Spotted you this morning. So much for taking my advice and going home. You and I are going to talk."

I muted the call long enough to look at Buzz and swear.

"It's okay," Buzz said, "he got lucky. Talk to him. Agree to meet."

I unmuted the call, saying, "When?"

"Now. Highbridge Road. It's between Flagler and Ormond. It's off of A1A," with that, Rex hung up.

I turned the blinkers on and spun the wheel, planning to make a U-turn.

"Keep going," Buzz said, pointing forward. "When we hit Main Street, take a right."

I did as instructed, Buzz explaining, "He's going to expect us to arrive from the coast, but we're going to take 95 north and approach from the other direction."

***

We got off Highway 95 at Old Dixie Highway, Buzz pointing out the turns to Highbridge Road. Above us, the gray sky and rain were blocked by overhanging oaks.

"Here's how we're going to play this," Buzz said. "First off, soon as he sees that you brought me along, his hackles will go up."

"Soon as I see his van, you duck down?"

As Buzz considered that, the narrow road twisted left, right and left.

"No, let him see you've got back up. Rattle him some."

Around a sweeping bend, the drawbridge came into view. I slowed to five miles an hour, scanning what looked like a park to the right with a dirt parking lot. No sign of the U-Haul. On the river, a white power launch was fifty yards from the bridge on the royal blue water. A loud bell began clanging from speakers up above.

"Dammit." I watched the steel grate roadway begin to rise twenty feet before us.

"No worries." Buzz was also scanning the opposite riverbank. "We're in no rush. I don't see him anywhere."

The drawbridge opened all the way, a tall barrier of steel between us and wherever we would find Rex from Texas. The white boat was gliding under when I heard a car door close from behind.

There was Rex; his van was parked twenty feet back. He had his gun out, and he was walking, stepping to his right so he was directly behind us.

"Buzz! He's behind us!" I shouted.

Buzz spun on his seat, cursing, fumbling with his seatbelt latch.

I went for the glovebox, for the Glock.

"Duck!" Buzz hollered.

The rear window exploded. There was no sound of the gunshot, Rex firing his silenced handgun. Glass sprayed over us as I got the glovebox opened. Another shot was fired. Buzz had his gun out, pulling on his door handle, screaming, "Unlock it," as he fought with the handle. I leaned back, Glock in hand, and hit the lock latch. The third shot took out the windshield. Doors unlocked, I turned on the seat, aimed at Rex and pulled the trigger, going for three shots. I got none. The safely was on. Buzz yelled in pain; his door flung open. I was splashed with blood from my right and didn't look. Instead, I mashed the accelerator to the floor and shifted into reverse. Tires burning, the car launched backward.

There was a loud thump and muffled scream of pain. From Rex or Buzz, I didn't know. The car bucked over what had to be Rex and crashed into the front of his van. The air was full of groans and yelling. I dropped the transmission into drive and mashed the pedal. Before we crashed into the raised drawbridge, I slammed on the brakes. Dropping into reverse again, I mashed the throttle, looking over my shoulder to aim. Rex had struggled up onto one knee, his gun hand out, empty, like he was trying to stop what was going to happen next. The rear of the Buick hit him straight in the face and chest. I didn't let up until we crashed into his van a second time.

The impact threw me hard against the seat, the back of the car trying to climb up the front of the van. I wasn't done. Back into drive, I burned the tires twenty feet forward. In the mirror was a prone Rex, not moving. It wasn't good enough. With Buzz groaning, leaning half out his door, I found reverse and blasted back over Rex a third time, hearing him strike and bash the undercarriage.

Sitting still, assuming he was tangled under the car, I was panting hard, listening hard as well. The Buick's engine sounded injured. Buzz was moaning. I turned to him, wiping the spray of his blood from my face.

Buzz had pulled himself back onto his seat.

"Hosp…" he breathed, his voice wet.

Hospital. Yes. Fast.

I glanced out over the hood. The bridge was lowering. I wanted to look him over, but it was more important to get him to an emergency room. As soon as the bridge was down, I raced us across. After a few more turns, and we were out on A1A, heading south. I had my foot to the floor, passing whatever we came upon along the two-lane highway.

Buzz became silent. I still hadn't looked at him. I kept the car blasting down the coast, thoughts screaming, trying to focus on where I had seen a road sign with an arrow pointing to "Hospital."

Halfway back to Daytona, I took my first glance. And wished I hadn't. His chin was to his chest, his shirt red was stained red. He had been shot in the right side of the head, where blood was still spilling. In his limp left hand in his lap was his useless handgun. His other was on the wound, as though it could contain that much injury.

We ran through a red light in Ormond Beach, horns blaring from both sides. I barely lifted. The sign with the hospital arrow came up, and I took a right onto Granada, seeing more lights to run. A mile along, we were climbing the long bridge from the island. As we descended into the city streets, Buzz let out a bark, splashing the dashboard crimson.

Buzz died with a sputtering of bloody bubbles and coughs.

Chapter Nineteen

Triage

Following the signs on the side of the roads, I pulled into the lot of Advent Health Hospital and made out the red "Emergency" sign above sliding glass doors. Parking right in front of the entrance, I climbed out and ran inside, finding the admitting desk, telling the woman behind it, "There's a guy out front. Seriously hurt. His head is bleeding bad."

"Where out front?"

"In the car. Please hurry."

She jumped into action, speaking a code into her headset that played out through the lobby speakers. That got three nurses walking fast for the doors, two men and a woman, one pushing a wheelchair. Looking at the young woman behind the desk, I read her name tag and said, "Thank you, Ms. Quan."

She nodded, typing on her keyboard.

The glass doors at my back slid open. I heard the nurses out beside the Buick, talking fast and urgent, one of the men shouting "Gunshot. Get me a gurney."

Hearing "gunshot," Ms. Quan looked up, not to me, but the beefy hospital security officer sitting at his desk off to the side. He was maybe twenty-five years old but walked slow and tired, like a man in his seventies. As the front door slid open, he turned to me, pointing, "Stay right there."

Buzz was rolled in under the care of the nurses, around a corner and into a room marked Triage. The security officer went out front and squatted beside Buzz's open door.

"You name, sir?" Ms. Quan asked. "Please take a seat."

"Jimmy Smith," I lied, still watching the officer out front.

"Your relation to the injured?"

"None. I was out walking…"

The officer stood and turned, entering with his eyes on me. Ms. Quan asked two questions. I didn't answer either, watching the big young man in uniform walk to me.

I dropped my eyes from his, pulling on a pained and confused face. His hospital security badge read Carlo Seinz.

"You are?" he asked.

"Jimmy—James Smith."

"What happened here?" he asked.

"No idea, Officer Seinz. I was out walking. Do that every day. Found him parked. Keys in the ignition. Figured it would be faster to drive him than call 9-1-1."

"Where did you find him?"

I paused. I didn't want to mention High Bridge Road and link Buzz to that crime scene.

"I'm sorry," I apologized for my confusion, "The parking lot at the Tomoka walk trail," I hoped there was one. "Is he going to be okay?"

I was doing my best unnerved good Samaritan act.

"Not mine to say. Have a seat over there." He pointed to the waiting room of modern couches and chairs. "Do not leave or wander off," he instructed.

He was looking me over with suspicion. Roles reversed, I would be too.

"Sure," I continued with the wide-eyed compliant act. Taking a seat, I waited until he had crossed the lobby and entered the triage room where Buzz was. When the door closed, I was up out of my chair.

Before the police could arrive, I got back inside the battered and blood-stained Buick and drove away.

***

Taking the back streets, I had enough of my wits to keep running north, the coast somewhere off to my right. I crossed the Granada bridge to the island and drove along the river a few miles before taking a residential street that led out to A1A. Twenty minutes later, I entered Flagler Beach.

My thoughts were swirling, not gathering themselves into coherence. I braved a glance at Buzz's side of the interior. Blood was everywhere but the clean fabric silhouette from his body pressed into the seat. There was a spill of the splattered documents he had climbed in with. Buzz was dead. So was Rex, the bounty hunter. And what was I to do about my part in that?

"Need to find a place." I scanned the condos and motels along the left side of the road. "Hid the car. Hide myself long enough to gather my thoughts."

Pulling into the Ocean Wind Hotel, I circled to the back lot, not seeing what I needed. Back on A1A, I drove another two blocks. I chose the Beachside Motel because it looked like it had rear parking. Driving to the lot around back, I saw what else I needed beside the garbage dumpsters. Climbing out, I took off my splattered shirt and walked over to the garden hose. Water running, I scrubbed blood from my face, hands, and arms. Leaving the Buick parked beside the dumpsters, I circled out to the front office of the motel.

The elderly woman behind the counter looked me over as I entered, her eyes to my hair. I might have missed a few spots.

"Vacancy?" I asked, drawing her gaze away.

"Always." Her eyes lost interest in me as she turned to her

keyboard. Her free hand placed a card and pen on the counter.

"Can I have a room out back?" I asked her after filling out the registration form, "I need some sleep."

"We can do that. Single, okay?"

"Yes."

"Room twenty-seven, nonsmoking. Ice machine is in the breezeway to the pool."

I thanked her and paid and exchanged the registration card for the key.

After unlocking my room out back, I unloaded the Buick: my briefcase and suitcase. Next was the papers Buzz had with him that morning, along with his handgun, also on the floorboard. Everything inside, I opened all four doors of the car and turned on the hose again.

After spraying the front seats and dashboard, I went to work with my bunched-up shirt, rubbing and scrubbing bloodstains, ignoring the pools they made under the seats. Climbing out, I dragged the hose to the rear of the car, where the battered trunk lid had broken free of the twine. It took me ten minutes to wash the last of Rex 's blood from the crumpled rear end. When I was done, there was an eddy of crimson and water around the car. I sprayed the pavement until the traces of red washed away forever down a storm drain.

Inside my room, I stripped in the shower and pushed my clothing and shoes into a garbage bag. Instead of showering myself, I put the bag by the door to get rid of it the next time I went out.

I sat naked in the chair at the window table.

I had killed a person in greedy, satisfying anger. Running Rex over *three* times, as I recalled.

There was little solace in having killed Buzz's murderer. The bounty hunter had been shooting at both of us. I had somehow been missed. But not Buzz. My newfound friend was lying in a hospital room, his life over forever.

"What do I do with this?" I asked the closed window blinds. Time to go to the police? Turn this over? They had the resources to find Kazu. Whereas I was on my own if I decided to continue the search. I'd be arrested or at least interrogated for my role. I had been behind the wheel all three times the Buick ran over Rex. One time could be explained, but the other two?

Temporarily pushing aside the decision to turn myself in, I stared at the thin stack of blood-dabbed pages Buzz had been carrying.

"You can wait," I told them.

I was in a downward spiral, not knowing what to do; how to accept the fact that I had killed. I got up and rounded the bed to the bathroom.

Sitting in the tub with the shower running, I rubbed my head, releasing a faint spin of blood around the drain.

"What do I do?" I watched the circling water around the drain until it ran clear.

Even if I didn't turn myself in, the authorities would undoubtedly link me to the car and Buzz and Rex. It didn't take a lot of imagination to see their skeptical faces as I attempted to explain the hunt for my grandson. And how do I protect him from them once they knew about his criminal past?

On their own, my pointer fingers touched as did my thumbs, and I raised them before my face. Blinking away the water running down over my eyes, I looked inside the viewfinder.

I received vignettes rather than a lucid story. My being questioned at a table in the police station. I blinked that aside. The death scene on the drawbridge came into clear focus, thankfully in black and white. Then came looking one time into the side mirror at Rex's crumbled body as I drove away. Buzz's final burbling death played, of course, there beside me in the front seat.

Blinking that away, I received a rare, screen-wide text—an oh-so-serious red question mark. Then my grandson's face superimposed and came into crisp focus as the question marked dissolved into sprinkling pixel dust.

I knew what I had to do. Not sure how.

Continue.

Buzz Guzman would want that, I hoped.

I received a glimmer, my first positive thought, warming the composition with warm white light. More theatrical writing rolled under the glowing image of Kazu's face.

He is no longer being hunted...

I stood in the tub and turned the shower off, my hands no longer linked. Climbing out, I dried off and dressed from my open suitcase.

I only had to find him.

Chapter Twenty

Urchins

I needed to find Kazu. Fast. But first, I had to gather my mind enough to make a plan. View finding wasn't what I needed. I pulled over the complementary motel notepad and pen and wrote "Next" across the top. Beside it, I added, "How."

Next – How

- No more Buzz Guzman, no Rhonda to lean on. On my own.
- The 7-Eleven. Convince that girl Feeb to help me?
- That strange walled home she pointed me to. Get inside?
- Walk that neighborhood with his photo?

There on the table were the printed pages Buzz had when he died. I added a bullet.

- Read whatever the reporter wrote.

"Start there," I told myself.

Sliding Buzz's gun aside, I took up the splattered pages. Blood had stuck them together but hadn't smeared the print.

Carson Staines – Photojournalist
Flagler Beach, Florida
Not sure of the date

Notes on the Hunt for Jappy the Killer – Continued

Know what Jappy wants? What he'll never get. A free life. His childish drawings. Surfing. A girlfriend someday. His murderous life forgiven and forgotten.

Know what Jappy is going to get?

All his fantasies and delusions smashed.

The insect is getting squashed. Stomped on and ground into the concrete. I'm very close to him now.

All that's left to do is spot him and his fellow street urchins. I know some of the places they like.

Last night, I learned about that Phoebe—Feeb—as the punks call her. With him hiding in the shadows like a cockroach, she is the key to drawing him out, with a dropped sugar cube. Seems those two have a thing.

This time I won't be trying to snare him. There's nothing more he can tell me for the story. Instead, it's time for some street justice. Soon as his story ends and he's nothing more than a stiff on the side of the road, I'll be far away. I'm smelling a book deal in this. Get my life back on the tracks. Cash fat and interviews and a condo on a beach.

All I have to do is keep my eyes and the car aimed on the prize.

Clearly, things didn't work out as Carson's Staines had planned.

All I learned was what I already suspected: convincing Feeb to help me was next.

The Buick started, engine running rough, but running. It was raining and there was no windshield to run the wipers across. I got the spool of twine from the back seat and secured the rear trunk lid again.

With the crunched and bashed windowless rental looking like it had been through a grinder, I stayed to the back streets of the beach town. The Buick's condition would be a red flag to any cop or sheriff I might come upon.

Turning onto 5th street, I parked one block back from the 7-Eleven, leaving the car in the sandlot at the back of a Mexican diner, off in the corner beside a stunted palm tree.

The sun would set in an hour or so. There would be darkness and shadows for her to hide in. I rounded the corner and walked the store windows, eyeing the dumpster first, seeing no loitering kids.

Stepping inside under the harsh lights, my eyes went to the counter first. No kids, no customers at all. There were voices to my left, two aisles back in the mini-market. One of her friends, the boy they called Slurp, was eyeing the corner display of jerky. I walked past him. There were two other kids in the last aisle.

Feeb was standing in the middle of the last aisle, that old beach umbrella over her shoulder, another girl at her side. Both were rain-drenched, no matter the umbrella. Their damp hair hung lifeless, their clothing soaked.

The other girl elbowed Feeb, warning, "Uh oh."

There was no need, Feeb had already spotted me, her lovely, bright eyes drilling into mine. She took a step back. The other girl ran up the aisle and turned for the doors.

"What do you want?" Feeb pressed, no fear in her eyes.

"You know." I took another step closer to her.

She stared at me, defiant, challenging. "You spooked him," her young voice full of confidence. "Never find him now."

The boy before the Jerky display yelled, "Run!"

Feeb flinched but saw it was too late for that.

I took her arm, saying, "Just a few minutes, all I ask. Help me find him… please."

"Let go." She looked at my hand on her arm.

"I will, soon as we're outside," I led her to the front of the store. With my free hand, I took out my wallet and flipped it open to the clerk behind the counter, saying, "Truancy," not waiting for a reply or worse a question.

Out front, I asked, "Are you going to run?"

"Haven't decided yet."

I let go of her arm.

"Have you seen Kazu today?" I asked.

She stepped off the sidewalk heading for the dumpster. I walked alongside.

"Let me see that wallet," she said.

I handed it to her and watched her flip through it—no badge or whatever she suspected.

"His photograph is in the back," I told her. "His mom gave it to me."

"His dead mom, you mean."

"She's very much alive and wants him home."

"Not according to Kazu." She took out the photograph. There he was, younger, smiling in his boat in the swimming pool.

"Aww," she sounded pleased, "he's like puppy sized."

We both studied the image, raindrops tapping it.

"Yes," I broke the spell. "Will you help me?"

Instead of answering, she put the photograph away and handed me the wallet. I pocketed it and she gave me the umbrella, saying, "Open it, please."

I did.

The warmth in her expression from the photograph dissolved.

She was back to eyeing me skeptically.

"Can you prove his folks are alive?"

I thought about that. It only took a moment to come up with the best way. "Would you like to speak to them?"

She turned away, pondering, looking out to the wet traffic on A1A.

"No need," she said, scanning the beach walk on the other side of the road. Cars were rolling slowly past, their headlights on, casting cones of light in the rain.

"There he is!" she yelped.

I fell for it, turning to see which way she was pointing.

Feeb ran. Fast and sure. Back across the front of the store and rounding the corner, leaving me holding her umbrella.

***

I went back inside the 7-Eleven and bought the latest *Daytona Beach News-Journal.* The headline read:

MYSTERIOUS DEATH ON DRAWBRIDGE.

Tucking the newspaper inside my shirt as I left, I headed back up 5th street to the Buick. When I was back inside my motel room, I opened the paper on the table.

Some reporter named Hank Fernandez had penned the front-page story, which ran under a color photograph of the crime scene on the draw bridge, taken from a distance, just back of the yellow crime scene tape, police and sheriff units blocking the view of the death scene.

The story was written in the best of crisp, direct telling.

MYSTERIOUS DEATH ON DRAWBRIDGE
By Hank Fernandez

> December 28th, 2018
>
> A dead body was found today, mid-span on the High Bridge Road drawbridge, an apparent victim of a hit and run. No identification of the victim is available, and no arrests have been made.
>
> Volusia County Sheriff Mick Graisse said earlier today that the unknown victim had died midday. A passing motorist called in the first report.
>
> When asked about foul play, Sheriff Mick Graisse refused to comment. Sources are saying that the victim was run over repeatedly. This clearly suggests a crime, not an accident.
>
> "We received a call at approximately 2:15 p.m.," McKnight said in a release. "And responded with all units. It's believed that a van found at the scene belonged to the victim and we are pursuing that as a source for identification."

There was more. A request for witnesses to please come forward, as well as a call out for anyone who had information to contact the sheriff's department.

I folded the newspaper and pushed it inside the garbage bag by the door, holding my bloodied clothing. The next time I left the motel, it would go into a garbage can at least a few miles away.

I was at a loss with what else I could do that night. Kazu was out there, somewhere. Driving the streets randomly wasn't a bad idea, but if any witnesses had reported the Buick, I would be pulled over fast.

"Walk the streets." I prodded myself up from the table.

And that is what I did until I was stupid tired enough for a few hours' sleep.

Chapter Twenty-One

Feeb and I

My phone woke me.

The curtains were gray with morning light.

It was my son, Bill.

"Hey, Dad, how's your search going?"

"I'm sorry, I 've meant to call you with the latest," I lied smooth and quick.

"Have you found him?" Bill asked hesitantly.

"No. But others have seen him. He's here. Just need to stop his running."

Silence, as there should be. Letting Bill absorb that news about his son. I waited until Bill broke the spell.

"I'm about to book my flight into Puerto Mita," he said, his voice raspy with emotion. "I'm coming alone. Can you pick me up, or should I get a rental?"

"Bill, I'm not in Mexico. Things changed."

"Oh? Where are you?"

"North of Daytona Beach."

"Florida? Okay, so I'll fly there."

I looked to the ceiling, searching for guidance.

"Son, this has turned ugly. I think it best you stay away."

"Is Kazu okay?" Bill measured out.

"Think so. It's the man chasing him that's caused all the trouble. He's out of the picture now."

"I'm coming. I should have done that earlier. I failed to believe enough."

"Be best if you stayed put; let me find out more."

I wanted my son nice and safe and thousands of miles away.

"Not happening," Bill said. "My next call is the airline. I'll rent a car."

It was pointless to argue. I changed the subject, hoping to lighten his mood.

"How is the dog doing?"

"Roadkill and Dan the Baby are thick as thieves."

I smiled at that image, hoping my son was doing the same. He must have, because he stayed off-topic with, "Dad, I have to ask. What's with the Jeep dealership?"

"Where's that from?" I asked.

"Been meaning to ask for some time. So?"

I closed my eyes and rolled back to a year and some before.

"It seemed like a good idea at the time. A clean and brightly lit place to hide and live whatever a normal life is."

"Well. You lasted a little over a year at that. Not bad."

We both grinned. I imagined his.

"Mom sent me us telegram about the upcoming divorce. Are you gutted?"

A not so safe question, but it was his to ask. Pauline was his adoring mom. I looked up to the ceiling before answering, "Close to that, yes."

"That hurts my heart."

"Yes, enough on that."

"I agree. Let's find my son."

We ended the call, Bill promising to call me as soon as he landed.

I sat at the foot of my bed, looking at my phone, mentally

changing gears, getting back to the main question.

"Where's Kazu?"

During the previous night's search of Flagler Beach, I walked the back streets of bungalows and cottages. The rains let up at two in the morning, and that's when I saw a single pack of jogging kids, no familiar faces, dashing across the grass plaza in the center of town. Sometime after, I gave up the hunt, stumbling tired back to the motel.

I could try to get inside the Maison de Danse place, convince the Aunt Izzie woman to listen, get her to open the gate.

"Feeb," I whispered, deciding she was a better bet.

Before I headed out to try and find her again, I placed another call—time to check on the hunt for Rhonda. Lance picked up on the third ring.

After the briefest of pleasantries, he said, "Something's breaking. No details yet. I'll call you soon as I know more. Have to run."

I showered quickly and headed out.

The weather was improved. Sunny blue skies and a light breeze off the ocean. There was an ATM at the Bank of America on A1A. I decided that maybe cold cash could persuade Feeb to help me. My card was declined.

Instead of wiping it off and trying again, I took out my old bank card from the Hollywood days and drew two hundred dollars. Now all I needed to do was find that young girl.

I headed back to the 7-Eleven.

Like the day before, I parked the Buick deep in the parking lot of the Mexican diner and walked up 5th street.

Five pre-teens were standing with their backs to the dumpster. I didn't see Feeb's face among them. I searched the store windows for her. Not spotting her, I started walking to the others.

"Look, dudes. It's that creep show," the kid Slurp said to the others. Being in a pack, they fed on their numbers, not running but offering a solid front. Five gangly kids in dirty clothes and battered shoes. Only the girl on the far right looked ready to scram, her skateboard poised for launch.

I stopped, took out my wallet, and fanned five twenty-dollar bills.

"Just a couple of questions and breakfast is on me," I offered before taking another step.

Their eyes roamed between the cash and my face. I put on my best friendly smile.

"Can any of you tell me where I can find Kazu?" I asked.

They were silent.

"Fair enough," I said. "You still get paid." I walked up to them.

The girl with the skateboard took off, pumping the pavement with her worn sneaker. The other four accepted one of the twenties.

"Last question, then I'll leave you. Promise," I said, the harmless buddy smile starting to hurt.

"The last twenty is for whoever can point me to Feeb. I have a hundred dollars for her, and like this, nothing else but a question or two,"

Slurp snagged the twenty, saying to his friends, "I'll split it with you."

Turning to me, he said, "We're going to watch you. You do anything pervo, we'll all be screaming for the police."

"That's fine. I only need a couple of minutes of her time."

"Feeb's working the beach. With the sun comes the tourists and their beach bags."

"She steals?"

"What planet you from?"

Ask a dumb question and that's what you get.

"Which beach?" I asked.

"Probably north of the pier."

At my back was A1A and a block up, the restaurant that fronted the Flagler pier.

"Thank you," I said, glad to lose the smile, listening to their foot pads as I walked across the parking lot.

With the sunny weather came a flock of rental cars and minivans with out-of-state plates. After crossing the two-lane highway, it was a hundred yards along the beach walk to the north side of the pier.

Leaning on the rail, I scanned. It was a different world down there—children shrieking with laughter, umbrellas and chairs and ice coolers forming islands of enjoyment. The surf was small and gentle and inviting.

Roaming my gaze from the pier pylons north, I looked for a sign of a young girl likely acting casual, strolling island to island, an eye out for beach bags left behind for a walk to the water.

Not seeing her, I looked as far north as possible. Best I could tell, she wasn't among the distance beachgoers. Turning back to the pier, I waited, hoping she would appear, walking from its shadow.

"Heard about the hundred. I get that first," Feeb said, her voice flat and defiant.

She was behind me.

"Agreed," I said.

"More questions about Kazu?"

"Yes. Questions, nothing more," I turned around, a smile back on my face. Taking out my wallet, I handed her the cash.

After counting it, she said, "Go on."

"When's the last time you saw Kazu?"

"Four days ago."

"Where?"

"Sandy's. It's an ice cream place. We both had banana." She twice folded the twenties and pocketed them.

"Any idea where he is now?"

"Maybe," her lips twisted, an adorable questioning, pondering expression. "Can I see the puppy photo again?"

It took me a moment to get it. I slid the photograph from

my wallet.

"That's where he lived? Looks nice," she gazed into the image.

"It is. A farm. With his mom and dad and baby brother."

"Kazu on a farm?" Trouble seeing that." Her smile expanded.

"His dad is headed down here to take him home."

"So you say." Her gaze hardened, rising to mine.

"All I want to do is let Kazu know. Nothing more. Tell him his dad is on the way and leave," I lied.

"You could try Nerdz."

"And what is that?"

"Comic shop on Moody, one block from here. Kazu's friend Ben runs it. Helps him with his ideas."

"Ideas?"

"His image-novels. Ben's helping Kazu with *influences.* I hung out with them two times.

"Could Ben be hiding him?"

"Doubt it, but he might have seen him recently. Far as I know, Kazu either sleeps at the dance house or April's garage."

"So I should check out the dance house as you call it?"

She shook her head.

"No. Waste of time. He's running again. Some man showed up at the dance house. A cop or someone. Scared Aunt Izzy bad."

"That would be me."

"Good job, mister."

"Agreed. Should I try April's garage, wherever that is?"

"You could try."

"Where is April's garage?"

"Next to her house."

Funny.

"Her place is a few miles south of here," Feeb revealed.

"Take me there?" I asked kindly as possible. "For another hundred?"

"Two hundred… and fifty. No. Three hundred."

"Okay, yes. We'll hit the ATM on the way."

"You have a bicycle? You don't look like a boarder."

"Neither, but I do have a car."

"If you want me to get in a car with you *after* I check it out, it'll be five hundred."

"Sure. And thank you."

Feeb looked up the beach walk to her friends, who true to their word, had followed me and were watching the girl and I closely.

"Be right back," she said. "I'm going to let them all know what I'm doing. Should take a half-hour, round trip. They'll be dialing 9-1-1 if I'm ten seconds late getting back. With your license plate number."

She crossed to the other kids. An argument broke out after she spoke. When it finally ended, she turned and nodded at me.

The other kids trailed Feeb and I up 5th street to the sandlot where the Buick was parked. I looked back as she and I stepped to the doors. One of the youths was scribbling fast on a scrap of paper.

"What happened to your car?" Feeb was clearly worried and hesitating.

A tornado? I thought to joke, deciding it was best not to. I told her the truth.

"There was this man chasing Kazu. He's gone for good now. But he busted up the car, trying to stop me from finding him."

I climbed in. Feeb did the same, much slower, eyeing my hands and me. I took the key out slowly and started the car.

She reached over and turned on the wipers.

"Why?" I asked, watching them sweep through the air.

"It's funny, duh," she quipped before launching herself over into the safer rear seat.

After getting her the promised five hundred dollars at the ATM, I asked," Where to?"

"Get on A1A south. I'll point out the turn."

"There," she said, three miles along. I braked and switched on the blinkers. There was no road sign, just a turn out onto a sand road running straight among wild dunes of palmetto, palm trees, and scrub brush.

Two hundred yards farther, she pointed to the right. "That's it."

I parked at the gate before a long sand driveway. Security cameras on steel posts turned onto the car from both sides.

"April doesn't let adults on her property," Feeb said.

"Who is April?" I asked.

"A *nice* adult. She has the garage set up with bedrooms with showers and door locks. Bunch of us stay here sometimes."

"Like a halfway house?"

"Without the bibles, yes. She even cooks for us. She's also Kazu's partner in crime, as she says."

"Partner in crime? What kind?"

"They have a credit card skimming thing going. He does the running for her."

I filed that away, hoping I was moving things along to Kazu's retirement from crime.

"You wait here," Feeb instructed.

I agreed. Farther back on the property was a modern, two-story white beach house with a detached garage to the left.

Feeb climbed out of the back seat and paused at my window.

"I'll go see if he's here. Let him get a peek at you after telling him your story. More likely than not, he'll *vamoose*."

While the cameras on both sides of the Buick stared me down, I watched the young girl walk up the white sand driveway and enter the shade of the breezeway. She opened the side door to the garage, opposite the tall white house.

I made a mental map of the route back there if I decided to approach April, the den mom. That seemed likely, but not yet. If I didn't get Feeb back to the beach in the allotted half-hour, I'd have the police on my tail.

Feeb reappeared two minutes later, closing the door, her head down. That said it all.

She didn't speak until she was back in the rear seat.

"Empty," she told me.

I nodded; what else was could I do?

Turning the car around in the driveway, I sped us back up the coast to Flagler Beach, to her waiting and worrying pals.

Before climbing out, Feeb patted the top of the seat between us.

"If what you're saying is true, I might want to help. Kazu, the farmer? I like that."

"It is true," I told her sincerely.

She opened her door and got out, her friends watching and studying her, each looking much relieved.

"Try the dance house," Feeb turned around long enough to say, "Maybe Aunt Izzy will listen. Doubt it, but what else you going to do?"

What else, indeed? I drove away, merging into the tourist traffic and taking the first right I came to so I could get the suspicious-looking Buick out from before so many eyes.

***

After knocking on the gate door in the stone wall for ten minutes, I stood in front of Maison de Danse, the camera tracking my movements but no electronic squawking or Aunt Izzy's voice from the speaker. Trudging back through the ivy, I returned to the car parked across the river road.

So began the rest of the day, every half hour knocking and waiting for a reply.

During one of my failed attempts to get Aunt Izzy to speak to me, I scaled the ten-foot wall again, this time getting a better look.

"What? Swim alongside the dead?" I dropped to the ground a few minutes later.

Two lengths of water, both fifty-meter lap pools, ran side by side in the compound. Lilly pads and green reed stalks decorated the lengths of clear blue water. Between them was what had to be a family plot. Mausoleums and slab memorials laid out in even rows, the oldest closest to where I hung at the top of the wall. Between them, the overgrown vegetation looked maintained, draping but not covering the white stone paths. At the back of the private cemetery, a row of tall, dense pine trees blocked my view of the grounds beyond.

Back inside the Buick, I gave up trying to make sense of what I had seen. Besides being strange, I struggled to figure out what had drawn Kazu to the place. And how he had found it. I shook off the thoughts—too many missing pieces of that puzzle for now.

Speaking of puzzles, I was running low on clues in my hunt for Kazu. I could return to April the den mom's place, introduce myself. Try that comic bookstore Feeb told me about. Both seemed like dead ends, but I was running out of leads, of ideas.

"Talk to me," I told the view of the gate in the ten-foot wall across the road.

My phone rang. It was Lance.

"Hey, Pierce. Those whispers about Rhonda? A goddamn false alarm. And an expensive one, so you know."

"What's next?" I asked.

"I dig and slog among these bad boys. I've got new calls out and some haunts I'm trying next."

"Okay. Good. Thank you."

"I'll keep you posted. We'll find her."

With that, we ended the call.

Twenty minutes later, I was knocking on the door in the wall—with the same result.

***

At four-thirty in the evening, I quit the "dance house," as Feeb called it. By then I had decided to lose the red-flag-waving Buick and get another car. A Willy, if possible.

"Ditch you first thing tomorrow morning," I explained to the nearly destroyed rental car. I turned around on the river road and headed back for my motel. It would be dark in an hour.

Returning to the Beachside Motel, I parked the car nose out in the back lot for two reasons. No rear license plate to be checked out and that side had the least damage if you ignored the missing windshield.

Sitting on the bed with another dinner in a drive-thru paper bag, I stared at my open briefcase of files and maps on the table and the bloodstained reporter's notes. Weary and frustrated, I decided to shower and head back out for another night of walking the streets of Flagler Beach. The death of Rex from Texas was my only success, of sorts, stopping his hunt for Kazu. But I was no closer to finding my grandson.

My phone rang.

"Hey, Pierce, it's Lance. Something's up. I found out who the goons who have Rhonda are working for. No full name, no phone number *yet*, but I'm on that. By the way, the police are doing their best, no knock on them. But this is a deep in the sewers job. No usual suspects, and their feelers don't reach as deep as mine. Also, I heard these bad boys are not local but from over the border. Hate to tell you, but that is even more alarming. They're known to play fast and deadly. That said, I'm confident money can grease open a door or two."

"Thank you," was all I could think to say. We needed to rescue Rhonda, and he was on that, which was the best I could do.

"Call me when you learn more." I ended the call. Important progress there, but I was mired in my hunt. Forgoing the shower, I left the motel to start a night of walking and looking and hoping, my spirits at a low ebb, but determined to do the best I could.

"Start with the 7-Eleven and then the tourist restaurants and shops along the beach. After that, the back streets."

He was out there, my twelve-year-old grandson. Running, hiding, and believing he was alone in the world.

Chapter Twenty-Two

Cellphone

The rains returned, bringing gusting winds under tumbling, angry gray clouds. As I climbed behind the wheel of the Buick the next morning, my spirits were also dampened, but I shrugged it off, telling myself, "Kazu's out there. All you need to do is persist."

During the night, there had been no news from Lance. I had failed to spot a single running pack of kids. Before falling into bed, I had drawn up a list for today:

1. Hit ATM and press Feeb some more
2. Hit the comic bookstore
3. Drive out to April's garage and bang on the door until she talks to me

The fourth bullet was a question, not answered because it could get sticky fast, especially if I was linked to the Buick used to kill Rex on the drawbridge. This last item was a last resort that I wasn't yet ready to think on until I had to; I would need to cook up a way to report Kazu's disappearance without getting myself thrown behind bars.

4. Go to the police for help.

After refilling my wallet at the Bank of America, I had no luck finding Feeb or any of her gang at the 7-Eleven. I crossed to the beach walk. With the winds and rain, the beach was abandoned. I watched the chaos of the waves at high tide exploding under the pier. After a few minutes, I turned away.

"Nerdz Comics." I looked back into washed out downtown Flagler beach. Entering the name into my phone for the address, I was interrupted.

"How did it go with Aunt Izzy?" The smirk in Feeb's voice said she already knew the answer to that.

"Big waste of time." I turned around. Her worn clothes were drenched, her hair hung in tangles, and she was smiling.

"That place is brain whack," Feeb said. "No idea why he likes it."

"Have you seen him?"

"Nope and it's day five. Like I said, he's gone under. Can't say I blame him."

"Right. I'm headed over to the comic store. Then back to the place with the garage."

"Know what you're doing?"

"Tell me."

"Spinning your wheels, stuck in the sand."

I wiped rain from my face.

"Probably, but outside of going to the police, I'm running out of ideas."

"Just a thought. Have you called him?"

Have you ever felt that first head shake after a deep sip of espresso? No more sodden me. I looked into her lovely eyes.

"No, I didn't know, never thought of that," I told her. "Do you have his number?"

"I don't have a cell phone." She shrugged.

What were the odds that he still used his original number

from years before?

I closed the display with the comic bookstore address on it and pulled up the list of my contacts. There it was, from years before, when his parents gave him his first phone for Christmas.

I hit call and put the phone to me ear. It rang nine times before dumping me to voicemail. A boy's voice, saying simply, "Kazu."

I left a message.

"Hello, Kazu… This is your grandfather, Pierce. I'm here in Daytona looking for you. Please call me back. I have news about your mom and dad and brother. Good news. Please call me. I'll buy you lunch or whatever you need… Again, this is Grandpa Pierce. I love you and want to help you."

I ended the call by reading him my phone number.

"There you go." Feeb was nodding, approving. "I'd call you back if I was him and heard that."

"Let's hope."

"No time for hoping. Know what I'd do next if I were you?"

"No idea," I said. "Tell me?"

"Find a techie who can hunt GPS or however they do it. Locate him that way."

"Feeb? You're brilliant. Thank you." I took out my wallet.

"Put that away. Kind of offensive. I want to find him, too."

I put my wallet back in my pocket.

"Anything I can do for you?" I offered.

"Keep on the hunt, is one. Keep your phone charged is two. Three, walk with me to Swillerbees."

"Sure. What is that?"

"Place with handmade donuts, one block up Moody."

We crossed A1A at the traffic light, Feeb saying, "I'll buy; I'm flush from yesterday."

I returned her smile.

***

Feeb and I shared a box with a half-dozen unglazed old fashions—her choice—and chocolate milk. My phone lay on the table between us, not ringing. She ate four of the donuts, and I finished off the other two.

"I'm leaving you to that." She pointed to my phone, wiping her lips with a napkin, and standing. I watched her leave, stepping out into the rain and wind, not caring at all.

I decided to pass on the comic bookstore and April and her garage. And no more knocking on the gate at the dance house. I watched my phone, willing it to purr and vibrate.

An hour passed. Nada. I bought a cup of coffee and sat, waiting, watching an occasional car pass along the waterlogged street, headlights shining through the rain.

When I finished the coffee, I decided to head back to the motel where I could watch the phone while it was on its charger. That's when it rang.

A text message. No name displayed. The number was blocked.

Heard you ran into Rex Thurges. A few times. No loss there.
You want the boy; you work with me. I'll find you.

Part Three

The Price

A man without money is like a bow without arrows

~ Indian Proverb

Chapter Twenty-Three

Declined

Back at the motel, I backed the Buick in by the palms and shrubs, hiding it as best I could. There was a note taped to my room door, red-stamped URGENT. Taking it off, I put the key in and twisted. It wouldn't turn. I read the note. It was official-looking, and a box was checked, the second item reading, FAILURE TO PAY.

The manager had scribbled a signature and wrote:

Your card was declined. Settle up now.

I broke into a cold sweat, even with the rain, feeling both confused and embarrassed. Instead of going to the motel office, I got back in the Buick and drove over to the Bank of America. Failing there, I found a PNC bank two blocks in from A1A. Same result – INSUFFICIENT FUNDS. On all three of my cards.

I counted the cash in my wallet, seeing I had enough to pay the fifty-six dollars for the night before.

I paid the balance due back at the motel and retrieved my belongings from the room: my suitcase and files, the phone charger, and Buzz and my handguns.

Sitting in the Buick, I started the engine. I had a half tank left and thirty-seven dollars to live on until the banking problem was fixed. In the past, a situation like this was resolved with a single call to Rhonda.

I turned the engine off—no need to waste fuel. I was about to call the first of the three credit card numbers. Instead, I put the phone down on the dash.

"That can wait," I told myself.

That text message. Sent by someone holding Kazu?

Rex was dead. I had seen to that. So who sent the message?

Until whoever *found me,* as the anonymous text said, I was supposed to do what? Sit on my hands and enjoy a rainy afternoon in Florida?

I climbed out, wishing I could lock up the Buick, what with my belongings on the back seat, but that was a cruel joke.

Pocketing my phone, I walked out to A1A, turning north for the 7-Eleven, not sure why, but it was better than just standing there in the rain.

I was out of resources to help me with the search for Kazu. I was also out of cash, and worse, out of ideas, save one. Shadow Feeb.

My clothing was soaked through to the skin as I stood at the corner of the 7-Eleven. My spirits sagged as well; no sign of Feeb or her friends, neither outside the store nor inside behind the plate glass windows.

Maybe it was time to go to the police? Tell them about my missing grandson. Get them to help and somehow not reveal that I was also the man who happened to have killed a bounty hunter? Was I smart and quick enough to pull it off? A shake of my head answered that.

I could hear waves booming along the beach right across the street.

A shadow formed over my head, and I heard the tapping of

rain on plastic. Turning, there was Feeb, holding her worn-out beach umbrella over both of us.

"You look like a drowned dog," she said.

"Feeling like one," I agreed. "Any chance you've seen him?"

"None of us have. So I'm guessing he didn't return your call? Course not, you're wearing your sad face."

Cars washed by on A1A, forming small waves to the curbs and gutters.

"Know what I'd do?" Feeb was watching the traffic as well.

"No, but I'd like to hear," I answered.

"Espresso. Get the brain and mood all lit up. Always works. Swillerbees is closed, but we could buy a couple of cans in there." She turned and pointed to the 7-Eleven behind us.

"Sure." I could afford a couple of cans, and a jolt did sound good.

Inside the store, there were no cans of espresso in the glass case, so Feeb went to the front counter and picked out a couple of tiny bottles of energy shots.

Outside again and under her umbrella, we both knocked back our shots of Blue Raspberry Extra Strength.

"That'll do it," she smiled, "Just give it a few and you'll be screaming ideas."

"Here's hoping."

While I waited for the chemical change to happen, three of her friends walked across the parking lot to us.

"I gotta run." Feeb stepped off the curb and headed to them. "I'll find you later. Or sooner, if I see him."

Watching her join her gang, I willed my phone to ring. Failing at that, I watched the four kids walk in a bouncy cluster of chatter until they disappeared around the corner. My thoughts turned again to go to the police for help with the search for Kazu. Maybe I could explain the death of Rex from Texas as self-defense? He had fired his gun, something Buzz Guzman and I hadn't done. The problem was, it was highly likely that they had analyzed the crime scene on the drawbridge and figured out I had run Rex over not once but three times.

"Maybe I could tell it, right?" I looked out across A1A to the lonely pier stretching out into the storm.

And maybe they would lock me up for a few days, saying they'll start a search for Kazu, but the priority was the murder and my role in it. And while I waited for their wheels to turn, there would be nothing I could do on the search in a jail cell.

"Not happening." I looked up into the tumbling gray clouds above. Rain pattering my nose and cheeks, either the hidden stars or the shot of Blue Raspberry Extra Strength spoke to me.

"Call Kazu again. Be more convincing. Describe the photograph of him in my wallet. Offer to meet in some crowded place."

I liked it. It was a forward movement. I took my phone out of my pocket.

I was scrolling through my saved numbers when the phone vibrated in my hand. An incoming text from a blocked number. I quit the search and tap opened the message.

> Cool your jets. No more sniffing around for you. If you want to see the boy again and not on a morgue slab, you'll listen to me and do everything exactly as I say.

I read it through twice. I was being waved off; I got that. What the text didn't say was that the sender had captured Kazu.

"Cool your jets," I reread. I knew of only one place I could do that.

Returning to the Buick in the back lot of the Beachside motel, I was wired from the energy shot. I climbed in onto the soaked driver's seat, fresh rain coming in through the missing windshield.

Was calling Kazu a second time *sniffing around*? Was I willing to risk that? If they had him, they had his phone. I pushed the idea aside.

So there I sat, mind racing, wheels spinning, but getting nowhere.

***

At sunset, I was still sitting behind the wheel, staring at my former motel room door, when the passenger door opened. I had heard no approaching footsteps.

Get the gun! my mind screamed. It was in the briefcase in the back seat.

I had been found, as promised. I swung around on the seat, my hands reaching for the briefcase, not looking at who had opened the door. I popped one of the latches, then the second.

There it was on top of the files. I grabbed it and, this time, remembered to take it off safety.

Swinging around, I pressed against my door and raised the barrel.

"*Geez*," a voice hissed. A young voice. Feeb's voice. "Don't point that at me."

"How did you find me?" I lowered the gun.

"Slurp did. Spotted your car and told me. I asked the motel desk for Dad's room number because I forgot. Tears helped. I was told you had been thrown out."

"Ran out of money," I said.

"Know that feeling."

"Why did you come here? Did you see him?"

"Can I have the back seat?" She ignored my questions.

"Sure."

"Thanks, and no, I haven't seen him."

"Dammit."

"Shouldn't swear around children," she smirked. "Came here because of the rain. I'm not hiking to April's garage and I'm not sleeping on the beach."

She knelt on the front seat and pulled my belongings onto the rear floorboard. Climbing into the back, she stirred around, trying to get comfortable, saying, "Lucky me. *My* doors still have glass."

"Get you some clothes out of my suitcase for a pillow," I offered.

"Thanks, but I'm good."

"Any chance you asked your friends to look for Kazu and let you know?"

"Done. What's your next plan?" she was moving about some more.

"Stare at my phone and wait."

"Not a bad idea. I know it's early. I don't care. Ni-night, Mister Pierce."

I turned on my seat, putting my legs across, wondering how I could sleep like that. Placing my phone in my lap, I reclined as best I could. If the phone rang, it would wake me, assuming I could find slumber.

***

At some point in the night, I sat up, my knees throbbing, as were my lower back and neck. The rain had stopped, and the air was cool. Best I could tell, I hadn't been dreaming. No strange story or struggles with the current chaos in my mind. Instead, there were two lingering images. The first, a young boy, Kazu, crouched in shadows, scared and cornered. The second was an all-knowing, sweeping white light, brushing the pavement back and forth, roaming closer, to within a foot of his battered shoes.

My hands rose on their own, thumbs to thumbs, pointer fingers touching, a few inches before my face. It helped to be half awake; I was too foggy to think. Instead, I gazed inside as a third image joined the other two, completing the composition. It was a baseball bat. I think it was in my hands. Either way, whoever held it had his back to Kazu, not interested in him at the moment. Instead, the bat swung hard, going for the source of the light and whoever was behind it.

"What *are* you doing?" Feeb asked from the back seat.

"Viewfinding," I answered.

"And that is?"

"Sometimes a way to figure things out."

"Is it working?"

"Actually, yes. I've been running down two roads at the same time."

"Is that possible?"

"No. And that's the point."

"You doing drugs, Mister Pierce?" she asked, amused.

"No need. This works for me," I explained.

"That's good. Some of my friends do. Turns them into monkeys. Ni-night again."

I had rarely used the viewfinder around others—no sense in setting myself up for ridicule or questions. Now Feeb had seen, and it had been okay. Looking at the collage and hoping it would meld into a short vignette, I waited to watch that bat connect and destroy the light on Kazu. It never did. I was patient, hopeful. After a couple of minutes, I realized why. The film was a suggestion, no, a push. The light couldn't be killed until I decided to take up the bat.

My hands came apart. I thought of the Glock in the briefcase in the back seat. Sometime later, sleep took me again.

Chapter Twenty-Four

Seagrass

Just after sunrise, my phone vibrated in my lap, waking me.

I swung my legs off the passenger seat, the phone falling between my knees. Scooping it up, I saw that text had come in. The return number was blocked like before. I opened the message.

> I have him. Can you still get inside your wife? Her finances?
> You better. Let's get together later today. Have ourselves a swap.
> Bring the wife's checkbook. I'll be in touch.

I read it twice, my eyes stinging from bad sleep, but my mind waking fast. Whoever it was knew my background, my links, my marriage to Pauline, and her finances. But, more importantly, they had Kazu.

Turning around, I saw that Feeb had taken off sometime earlier. I pulled my briefcase up over onto the passenger seat and opened it. There was my 9mm, waiting for me to decide to pick it up.

I knew it was baseball bat time. Knock that bright searchlight out of the park. But I paused. I had already killed once. I thought that was something I could live with, considering the circumstances. So, it wasn't picking up the gun that caused the hesitation. It was the other question—wouldn't it be better to pay off whoever? Get Kazu first and turn all of this over to the police? That felt right. I closed the suitcase and climbed out.

Stretching my sore muscles beside the car, I realized it was time to call my soon-to-be ex-wife. With my finances frozen or emptied or whatever, I needed to ask her for money, something I had never done during our many years of marriage. She loved our sons and grandkids as much as I, so it was a matter of pushing my pride away. I decided I could do it and, with that, realized the call would have to wait until I knew the price for Kazu's release.

That's when my phone rang. It was on the dashboard, and I climbed in for it, bumping it away, my greedy finger missing. The phone slid across and tumbled into the passenger floorboard. I circled to the other door and scooped it up fast. But not fast enough.

New Voicemail displayed.

I hit play, the phone pressed to my ear.

There was a clattering. No words. Only rustling movements. Seven seconds long.

Playing it back, I heard nothing new.

Frustrated with myself for screwing up, not getting the phone in time, I hit replay a third time.

As the call with no words played, I recognized Kazu's number.

When I tapped replay again, the phone went black. The battery dead.

"No, no. Not now," I pleaded.

On the passenger seat was the open briefcase. I had the charger but no outlet in the Buick to plug it into.

Pocketing the phone, I left the motel. The rain had returned; no winds, but a steady, heavy downfall. Out on A1A, I jogged to the right, for the 7-Eleven a few blocks away.

None of the kids or Feeb were out front, and that didn't

matter; I was on a different mission. Inside, I paid out seventeen of my remaining thirty-seven dollars for a car charger: all I needed to do was breathe some life back into my phone.

Running back up the sidewalk to the Beachside Motel, I ignored the rain striking my face. I had the charger in my hand and only needed to plug my phone in and wait for the next text or call from Kazu or whoever had my grandson.

I ran past the motel office door, my head down, and crossed the pool deck for the back lot. Going out the gate, I turned for the Buick parked nose out, hidden as best I knew how.

I stopped running, my shoes splashing in a wash crossing the lot. Raising my hand for a shield for my eyes. I stared, disbelieving.

The Buick was gone.

***

The elderly woman behind the counter in the motel office watched me enter, squaring her shoulders and tacking on confident, daring eyes.

"Hello," I offered, friendly, hoping to thaw her some. "My car is missing. By any chance, do you know—"

"We're not a parking garage. You want that wreck, call Flagler Towing Yard," she looked comfortable facing deadbeats down.

"Do you have their number?" I don't know why I bothered.

"Nope," she dismissed me by closing a binder and looking over my shoulder and out the window.

Well, that was that. I turned and went back out in the rain. My car and all my belongings were gone—no funds to retrieve them.

No sense hanging around the motel, the manager would likely call the police about a vagrant and loiterer: me. I went out to the street and crossed to the beach walk alongside the restaurant fronting the Flagler Beach pier.

What to do with a dead cellphone? There had been many times in the past when I had mocked people's attachments to those silly electronic devices. Now a life depended on my getting it working again.

"Time for begging," I told myself, not for coins but electricity.

I looked reasonably sane and not too much like a bum. True, my clothes were badly wrinkled, and I needed a shave, and my hair was wet and a riot. Straightening my shirt front with one hand, I used the other to finger comb the tangled mop on my head. While the beaches were empty because of the rains, the Rusty Pelican was drawing customers.

With an embarrassed expression and polite words, I began approaching departing diners.

"Excuse me, sir…" got me nothing for more than an hour. One glance at me and the charger in my hand was the last look I got.

The restaurant hostess came out and told me to leave or she would call the police.

I agreed but didn't leave. Instead, I moved ten yards from the doors, along the sidewalk where customers had parked at the curb.

A retired couple took pity on me. They we dressed in their tropical best, looking to be in their seventies. The man gave me his skeptical eyes when I approached him.

"Sorry to bother you, sir," I said. "My phone died. My wife has the car. Could you charge it for me so I can call her?"

"Veteran?" he asked.

"Yes, sir," I lied.

While I stood on the beach walk, he took my phone up inside their RV.

***

With the phone breathing again, I saw I had a new message from my son Bill. Had he arrived in Daytona? I had forgotten about his arrival. That voicemail had to wait, as would the second from Lance with a likely status on his search for Rhonda.

There were no new texts from whoever had Kazu. I reread the last message. It said nothing new to me. I was at a loss for what to do next except wait until I was contacted again. I sat down on the bench farthest from the restaurant doors, under an awning. With my phone in my hands, eyes to the splashing cars passing in both directions, I decided to listen to the two voicemails from Bill and Lance.

The phone purred as I scrolled—a new text. Forgetting the voicemails, I opened it.

> We're going to have ourselves a swap meet. Tonight. I'll let you know where and when.

That was it.

I needed more. Could I send a reply to a blocked number? I decided to try, typing:

> Is Kazu okay? You haven't told me how much money to bring.

No reply for the next slow, breathless minute. Then:

> He is "okay," and three hundred thousand will get him returned to you.

I stared at the text. Three hundred thousand. I had, what, sixteen dollars and change?

I knew what I had to do next and stalled. I looked up along the street. The rain had stopped, replaced by a white mist with no wind. The temperature was climbing and the sun was a hazy white bulb high overhead. "No other options," I said to the sky.

Pulling up Pauline's number, I called.

"Hey, you," my soon to be ex-wife greeted me warmly and softly.

"How are you?" I sincerely wanted to know, no matter the mess I was distracted by.

"Fine. Busy. Doing the prep for the next work," which meant she was immersing herself in the ways and details of the next film character she would be portraying. "You doing okay?" she added.

"Yes. In a bit of a bind. I need…" How do you hit up your wife for a loan, something I had never done?

"Need what, Pie?" she asked nicely, sounding concerned.

"I'm calling about Kazu."

"Oh… Why?"

"I've been searching for him, and—"

"What? Pie? Are you sober? Please tell me you are."

"I am."

"Then you're confusing me. Did you take a blow to the head or something?"

"He survived," I said and held my breath, pretty sure I knew what would come next.

It did.

"Oh, Pierce. You and your crazed pursuits. What is this really about? The divorce? We've talked this over so many times."

"No, not the divorce. To free him, I need to borrow some money."

"How much money?"

"Three hundred thousand," there, I got it out.

I could see her beautiful gaze, calculating, processing, her lovely eyes surely off into the distance. She took a moment before replying.

"Have you signed the divorce papers?" she asked gently. "Your settlement will easily cover that."

"I'm going to, you have my word. All I need is another set sent to me."

"Lost them again? Pie? Every day passing only makes all of this the sadder."

"Yes. It has taken me too long to accept. But I have." That was true.

"Then there is your money. Why did you call?"

"Timing."

"Help me with that? What do you mean?"

"I need the money… today."

"To free Kazu, as you say?"

"Yes," I answered, hearing the skepticism in her tone. Without explaining what I had been doing over the past week, all that I had learned and done, I deserved it.

"I'll call the lawyers. Not sure how long it will take, but I'll press. I won't ask again if you've been drinking, but I will ask you to fulfill your promise to sign and send the divorce docs."

"Thank you. And I will, soon as I find my car." Of course, I probably shouldn't have said that.

"My darling, Pie…" she whispered. Was it disappointment? Pity? Or just weariness with me? Surely, her head was shaking.

"Thank you again," was the best I could offer. "When he's free, I'll have him call you."

"That would be a dream. Now go find your car."

We ended the call minus our once-loving endearments.

Crossing the street, I walked to the 7-Eleven to buy a newspaper to read the latest on the drawbridge murder I had been a large part of. There were a few copies of that morning's *Daytona Beach News-Journal* in the rack. Seeing that the story had slid under the fold, I felt too disheartened from the call with Pauline to buy a copy. Instead, I bought something very cheap to eat and drink, even though I wasn't hungry.

Leaving the store, I saw Feeb's friend, Slurp, walking alone across the parking lot. I went to him, pasting on a friendly, casual smile.

"Can I bother you for a second?" I asked.

"Already have," he didn't slow up, and I turned as he passed by. He was confident for a boy not yet a teen.

"Just a quick question," I said.

"Buy me a lemon-lime?"

"Sure. How much are they?"

"Three dollars, and I keep the change."

I took out three ones and handed them over.

"Be right back," he said over his shoulder and went in through the door.

When he stepped out, he held a jumbo-sized Slurpee, straw in his mouth, pulling hard on it.

"I need to hide for a while, until tonight. Any ideas?" I asked him.

One of his eyebrows arched. He stopped sucking on the drink.

"Police?" he asked.

"Yes. I'll have everything straightened out tomorrow."

"Sure, you will."

"I need somewhere safe and quiet. To make a few calls and not be bothered," I tried to look my best non-criminal.

"It's not supposed to rain." He was looking out into the street.

"Meaning?"

"You can't stay in our camp, but you could hide nearby, not too close."

"Sure. A safe distance, no problem. Where?"

He pointed to the beach beyond the passing traffic.

"North of the pier. The seagrass."

Chapter Twenty-Five

Swap Meet

Climbing down the sandy embankment of palmetto and scrub weeds, Slurp led the way another seventy-five yards up the beach. We walked without talking. He was still working on his Slurpee as I followed with my cell phone in hand.

Their camp was a pile of boards taken from storm destroyed beach stairs. Two kids were digging a fire pit, a girl with a shovel and a boy using his hands. They were hidden from the beach by the high grass around them.

"Stay here. We don't like adults." Slurp pointed to the white sand twelve feet away from the others. He went on ahead, calling out, "Permission to enter."

It must be an inside joke. The other kids didn't reply. The girl with the shovel turned around to him.

"Who's that man?" she asked, voice full of suspicion.

"Someone trying to help Kazu. He's not truancy or police."

"Sheriff?" she asked, looking me over.

"Not that either. He also knows Feeb."

"He can't enter."

"He knows that."

"Got any newspaper?" She either forgot or accepted my

presence.

"And a Bic." Slurp swung his backpack around to his side and unzipped it.

I sat on the sand and looked to the waves washing up the beach in the low tide. After checking my phone and seeing I had four out of five bars of power, I rested my head on my crossed arms and closed my eyes.

I should call Lance the investigator back and check on his progress. Should I return Bill's call? My son was somewhere in the area, wanting to help with the search. Instead, I waited for my phone to buzz, willing the person who had Kazu to text me, telling me how I could get him back.

At sunset, three more kids entered the camp. Neither one was Feeb as I had hoped. Their beach fire was lit, the burning wood cracking. They sat in a circle around it, chattering. Sometime later, I overheard one of the boys say, "Really hungry."

"I have ten dollars left," I called over to them. "Use it, go buy something to eat for everyone."

That got them all to their feet. Slurp was chosen to go to the Dollar Store.

The half-moon rose out of the Atlantic, a dull bulb because of the fog. The tide rose and waves broke in a constant rhythm.

When Slurp returned from the market, he was greeted warmly. He carried a plastic family pack of hot dogs and a can of beef stew. They yakked and kidded while cooking their meal and ate in ravenous silence.

At ten o'clock, my phone buzzed. The message was straight to the point.

You have the money?

If you'll take a debit card, yes.
I typed my reply.

We can work with that.

Where are we doing this? I typed.

The swap meet? I'm liking
the scene of your last crime.

The drawbridge? I don't have a car.

Get an Uber.

I'm out of cash.

Have yourself a nice walk.

When?

3 a.m., nice and quiet.

Staring at the exchange, I waited for anything more. There was none.

"Slurp? Can you help me? Just take a minute?" I called over to the camp.

He joined me, reluctantly. I held my phone up to him. "Does this have an alarm clock?"

"Of course. What time you want?"

Good question.

Seven miles, I guessed. Ten minutes a mile by foot.

"One-thirty. Just in case I nod off."

He worked the icons on the phone and handed it back without a word. I watched his silhouette return the low burning fire.

The waves exploding on the beach marked the passing time. Returning my forehead onto my crossed arms, I closed my eyes, the phone in my lap. I never slept.

***

At the edge of Flagler Beach, I walked the coastal jogging path alongside A1A. The empty and dark beaches were to my left and hotels and restaurants to my right. Coming upon a row of condominiums, I paused for a breath. I had left on time so I could afford it, standing there sweating and looking farther up the road.

The next handful of miles were along the untamed wetlands fronted by sand knolls of thorn brush. I didn't see any headlights running the highway in either direction, just the fog-heavy night. Thirstier than tired, I looked to my right.

Across a lawn was a condo with a row of open-air patios, each with its own ocean view. I studied the ones with their porch lights left on. I didn't spot a curled water hoses, but something else spoke to me. Leaning against the side wall of Unit Nine was a cream-yellow bicycle with fenders and a wicker basket.

Within minutes, I was back on the jogging path, pedaling at a good clip.

"Murderer, hobo and bike thief," came to mind. It was almost funny.

***

Taking the turnoff onto Highbridge Road, I slowed up. As I recalled, the bridge was a half-mile up around a bend. I had no idea what was going to happen next. I climbed off the bike and set it on the sand alongside the two-lane.

What I wanted as I walked forward was the gun inside the briefcase inside the impounded Buick, assuming all my belongings hadn't been stolen or pawned. What I had was my cellphone and the bank cards in my wallet.

Bank cards. That stopped me right there. The phone still had three-quarters of a charge. I did a search on the Hollywood bank, believing that was the account Pauline would have the three hundred thousand moved to. It was fifteen minutes to three in the morning. Should be enough time. I tapped on the bank's customer service icon, then on the phone number display.

After wandering their electronic rabbit trail of pre-recorded prompts, I got a young man on the line. Before he could tell me my balance, I answered his painful list of security questions. Even at that late hour, he was trying to be pleasant and caring. I played along, moving foot to foot, impatient. He put me on hold. I stared up the road.

"Mr. Danser, I regret to inform you, your account is overdrawn."

I ended the call without a word. I was walking into who knew what without my side of the bargain. Instead of texting them with the bad news, I continued up the road and around the bend, to the view of the drawbridge over the black river.

There was a service hut under a lamp at the base of the bridge, its windows dark.

Walking out onto the steel grating, the river below showed in the gaps in the steel grating. I had the bridge to myself. No voices, no vehicles parked along its length.

Stopping mid-span, I turned and looked for any sign of life from behind. A glance at the phone said it was a minute before three.

I heard the car before I saw it, its exhaust throaty, even at just a few miles an hour.

Headlights rounded the turn before the opposite side of the bridge, illuminating the trees along the side. When they came fully into view, the high beams were switched on, forming two glares of white light in the fog from the river below.

The car drew to a stop thirty feet from me. I stared into the blinding headlights, two odd shapes, almost familiar. The driver's door opened. I couldn't see who I was facing, listening for the other doors to open as well. Whoever it was had come alone. Well, hopefully not alone, but with Kazu.

Frightened, but not about to give that away, I spoke first.

"Where is he?" I shouted.

"Have the money?" came back. He or she was using one of those kid toys that garble your voice, so it sounds like a robot.

"On the way. Let me see him."

"You're kidding, right?"

"I'm having the money moved. I'm good for it."

"But not right now."

I didn't answer that. "Show him to me," I called across. If he killed those high beams, I might get a glimpse of Kazu.

"Not happening."

"Is he okay?"

"Get your shit together. You've got exactly *one* last chance before he's handed to the Mexicans. You'll hear from us about the when and where."

Was Kazu really inside the car? Gagged and bound with rope in the back seat? Duct tapped in the trunk?

"Show him to me!" I shouted, walking forward. "Show me he's all right!"

The car door closed. The engine started. The headlights receded into the mist, backing slowly across the bridge and into the night.

Chapter Twenty-Six

The Big Guns

I walked back along High Bridge Road to where it emptied onto A1A. North or south, did it really matter? I retrieved the bicycle even though the last thing I needed was to be pulled over riding a stolen, cream-yellow single-speed.

I chose to head south. Even though Flagler Beach was closer, my son was staying somewhere in Daytona Beach. Riding in the dulled darkness that only four the morning provides, I pedaled along the coastal walking path.

An hour later, I was drenched in sweat, breathing taxed, knees screaming. Climbing off and walking the bicycle along the side of a store advertising "TEN THOUSAND T-SHIRTS!" I turned on their garden hose. With cold water running from the top of my head to my shoes, I cooled off, pausing to take deep gulps. I needed a real shower. I was smelling ripe. I wanted a motel bathroom for a long rinse, soap and shampoo while coming up with a new plan while I sat on a shower pan.

Turning off the tap, I rubbed the stubble on my face and looked out onto South Atlantic Avenue. There was no traffic except a garbage truck stopping and starting on the far side of the four lanes. Sitting with my back to the wall, I took out my phone.

Bill's last voice mail played:

"Dad, what the hell? Why haven't you called me back? Are you okay? I'm here at the Holiday Inn. Tell me what I can do to help find Kazu. I'm going to wait another hour and then I've got to act. I'd rather talk to you first, but… I've got an idea. Love to run it past you. Call me, please."

He had an idea. I wished I did too. Sitting in a puddle forming around my drenched clothing, I searched the phone for directions to his hotel. No matter the hour, I needed to know what he was planning to do.

Mounting the bicycle again, I pedaled out to the street and turned south. According to my phone, the Holiday Inn was a mile and a half away.

Leaning the bicycle against the wall beside the hotel entrance, I decided to call Bill first instead of approaching the front desk looking like a half-drowned alcoholic, doubting I'd be given his room number in that condition.

He picked up on the second ring.

"Dad? Where are you?" he asked, his voice was worried and wide awake. Not surprising. He lived on a farmer's clock.

"Downstairs. Give me your room number?"

"Three-twenty-two, but Dad, I'm not there."

"Where are you?"

"I waited and waited for you to call me."

"Yes, I'm sorry about that."

"Would have run this past you but had to do something to find Kazu."

"Where are you?" I repeated.

"Volusia County Sheriff's Office. I filled out a missing person's report, and I'm waiting for the officer to return. We're going to go over the report. Kazu's story is hard to explain."

So now the authorities were on hunt as well. Or would be, as soon as they were done interviewing my son.

"Dad?" Bill broke the spell.

"Yes, I'm here."

"I hope you're okay with this?"

I had a brief selfish flash. He mentions me and they run a check. Tie me to a rental car. Tie the car to the murder on the drawbridge. No matter, I pushed that aside.

"It's a great idea. Long overdue," I told my son. "I was hoping to find him on my own, but they have triple the resources."

"Yes? That's a relief. If I can, I'm not going to say anything about Mexico. I'm telling them he simply ran off."

"That's best. Good thinking. Don't need them looking into all of that."

"Agreed. What are you up to? Why don't you drive over and join me here?"

"Wish I could. You'll do fine. I have some things I need to take care of."

There was no way I was riding the bicycle over to the sheriff's department. They were the last people I wanted to talk to.

"Sure," Bill said. "Let me know how I can help? I hope to be out of here in an hour or two."

Bill was called away by a male voice in the background. We ended the call.

***

Frustrated and now threatened because of the sheriff's involvement, I ditched the bicycle behind a shrub. I walked up the street to a beach entrance. Finding a bench facing the Atlantic, I turned to what was important. Rescuing Kazu. I took out my phone. Sunrise was coming from somewhere over the ocean. The eastern sky was the color of pewter under the black of night.

I called the numbers on the back of all three cards. There were still no funds transferred to the Hollywood card. Same with the other two. This wasn't like Pauline. I was sure she had done her part. Something had happened to my accounts. When I asked, I was told to call back during normal business hours.

My shoulders sagged. It wasn't from being up all night.

"You and your windmills…" I chastised myself.

Bill had known what to do, the best thing to do.

"Suck it up," I told myself. "Turn yourself in. You have a lot of information they could use."

Entering "Sheriff" into my phone for the address, I paused before launching the search. I opened Lance's last voicemail, clearly stalling.

"Sorry, Pierce, it was another false lead on Rhonda. Now there's nothing on the streets but silence. This quiet isn't good. When the rats scurry, it most often means something's happened that they want no hand in. All that said, I'm not giving up. She's out there and we are going to find her. There are two Mexicans I'm going to press over in Santa Monica. I'll keep you posted."

I had dragged Rhonda into this and where had that got her?

My finger was still on the search button when the phone purred. I opened the incoming text.

> Last chance, Mr. Danser, before he is tossed over the
> border to those murderous thugs.
> If you don't pay out, his tongue comes out.
> His hands come off.
> Mess up again, and, well, you can visualize that—
> if you've got the stomach.
> They'll still take him, minus a few parts.
> You've got seven hours to pull the money together.
> We'll let you know where.

Best thing to do next was to take that and the other texts to the sheriff. I had seven hours and not a penny to my name against the three hundred thousand.

I tapped the phone, and the directions to the county sheriff's headquarters appeared. I retrieved the bicycle. It was a thirty minutes' ride away. I began constructing how best to tell all I knew, deciding to start with the current situation and work back. The seven hours were ticking away. Windmill chases were over. It was time to join up with the big guns, as they say in the movies.

The phone vibrated in my pocket as I climbed onto the bicycle. Tempted to let whoever wait until I reached the sheriff's office, I pulled it out of my pocket.

I recognized Rhonda's number and answered.

"What's the latest on the search for Kazu?" she asked, her voice calm and curious.

"Wait! What? Are you okay? Where are you?" I'm sure I shouted.

"Snug as a bug. Eww, scratch that, bad visual. I'm safe and sound."

"Are you sure? How did you get away?"

"Save that for later and yes, I'm fine. Did you find him yet?"

"I'm so relieved you're okay."

"Got that. Now, tell, please."

Telling her about the mess I had made of things could wait. Instead, I said, "He's alive. Here in Florida."

"Well, ain't that the tits? How can I help?"

"By going home and letting your parents know you're safe. Then you stay there and heal up."

"Deal. Then what?"

"That's all you're going to do."

"Calming my folks down and healing is going to take about a half hour."

"Rhonda, no. Take a week. Book a cruise or whatever you like to do to recover."

"Gee, that sounds cheery. But it's not happening."

She was interrupted by questions from a female voice.

"No need," Rhonda told the woman.

"Pie?" she returned to the call. "So?"

"Take a long bubble bath. Order dinner in. Get some sleep. Book a vacation. I'm buying."

"Another half hour wasted. You didn't answer my question."

"There is one thing. My banking is hosed. After you're doing okay, can you look into it?"

"Your banking is always hosed," she smirked. What a lovely sound.

"Pauline sent over a deposit. I just can't find it."

"So… That means you signed the divorce docs? Sorry, none of my beeswax."

"Not yet. She's helping me with… Kazu's ransom."

We were both silent with that, which was rare for the two of us.

In the background, more voices were talking to her. I heard, "Go with the EMCs."

She ignored them.

"Pie?"

"I'm here."

"Soon as I'm done with this dog and pony show, I'll go home. Fire up the computers and phones. Find your money. Repair you accounts. I've got to run, but I'll call you back in a few."

"I'm not sure how to thank you." My eyes were closed, my chin down.

"Yes, you do. Save him."

Chapter Twenty-Seven

No Moola

"Hey ya, Pie," Rhonda called me back a minute later.

"Where are you?" I asked.

"Warehouse district in Santa Monica. Cops all over the place. I'm sipping a delicious *chilled* bottle of water in the front seat of a cruiser."

"How did you get away?"

"Someone stopped feeding the dogs."

"Explain?"

"The guy they called the cowboy stopped paying the expenses. After waiting twenty-four hours, they simply left. Much less than pleased."

"Did they harm you?"

"Neither hide nor hair. Their apartment was a pigsty, but they left me alone."

"They just walked away?"

"Yep. No moola, so off they scurried."

The "cowboy" had to be Rex from Texas. Dead Rex from Texas.

"I got out; those guys didn't even lock up," Rhonda explained. "Called 9-1-1, and here I am, sitting in the sun, all safe and sound."

More than relief, I was lifted, knowing she was safe and okay.

"I'm so sorry I dragged you into all of this," I offered what I knew was going to be the first of many sincere apologies.

"Pie? I stepped in on my own, eyes wide open. You know that."

Closing my eyes, I thanked the stars above. She was unharmed and free.

Chapter Twenty-Eight

Zack

Deciding to leave Bill to help the sheriffs find Kazu, I climbed onto the bicycle, no idea where to go next.

I'm staying the course. I pushed off and started pedaling along the sidewalk in front of the towering beach hotels. A half-hour later, I turned into Tom Renick Park, where there was a beach entrance with a parking lot and picnic tables with a view of the beach below. I didn't need the vista; I needed the outdoor showers.

With the dismal weather—boiling clouds and rain and wind—I had the park to myself.

I was exhausted and groggy from lack of sleep, and that had to change. I learned that with each push of the shower tap, I got a minute of lukewarm water. My chin raised, I washed and rubbed my hair and face with my hands. After hitting the tap seven or eight times, I was drenched, clothes and all. It wasn't a private tub where I could sit and make a viewfinder, but it had to do.

If Rhonda worked her magic, I could make the exchange happen. If for some reason she couldn't, I had six hours to think of a new stall.

Stepping out from the shower, combing my hair with my fingers, my next step came to me. If the three hundred thousand didn't appear in my account, I needed a weapon. Off to the side of the playground was a plastic crate labeled Lost & Found.

I scanned the beach railing for any loose steel bars. I had no luck with that; the park was well maintained.

I walked over to the Lost & Found tub.

"Maybe some kid forgot his 9mm?"

There were buckets and beach towels and a shovel, but it was made of plastic. I saw lots of flip flops and rusted beach chairs. I dug deeper, not sure why, and hit pay dirt.

A child-sized aluminum baseball bat, all nicked up with pink grip tape.

It was ridiculous and ineffective, and it fit in the wicker basket hanging from the handlebars. It was a start until I found something else dangerous and threatening.

My phone vibrated, and I pulled it out. It was them.

Tell us you're not stupid enough to have talked with the sheriffs? Someone lit them up.

Not a word, I replied.

We might believe you. With your hands in Rex's killing, they would have taken away your phone before throwing you in a cell.

His father went to them. He doesn't know anything about Rex or what we're doing, I typed.

Hate to hear that. It clouds the waters.

But we're good? I asked.

Of course. Cops are still filling out forms, I'm sure.

Can you tell me where we are going to meet? I need time to get wherever. I still don't have a car.

Zacks.

Who/what is that?

Put on your thinking cap.

Is Kazu okay?

1 p.m. Don't bother showing if you don't
have every last penny of the three hundred k.
We bought a new power saw.

The call ended. The battery was half-drained. I dialed the 800 number on the back of my old Hollywood card.

In addition to the three hundred thousand, there was five hundred sixty-one dollars left in the unfrozen account.

I called Rhonda.

"You are brilliant as always," I greeted her.

"I know that, but thanks. Who's this Lance dude? He pounded on my front door."

"I hired him to find you."

"Well, please fire him. Nice enough, all bugged-eyed to see me."

"Good as done."

"How's the hunt going?"

"I'm close. Now that the money is there, the last step is the exchange."

"When's that?"

"In a few hours."

"Well, that's a rocket. Yay you."

"Yay *us*."

"What can I do to help?"

"Take your bubble bath. Pour yourself a glass of champagne. Unplug from all of this. You've been through too much."

"That's going to happen, just not yet. So you know, your credit rating has gone down the toilet and your banks are all defensive about who froze your assets. Any idea?"

"Yes, but that has to wait." I suspected Rex from Texas but didn't know.

"I agree. Time for you to focus, zoom your camera on your grandson. Get him. End this nightmare."

"Yes. It ends today. Got a new idea. As soon as I have him, I'll let you know."

Ending the call, I did another search. Not on "Zacks," whatever that was.

My next stop was an eleven-mile bike ride away.

***

Backed up to the river and circled with a cyclone fence, Flagler Towing Yard was on an unnamed dirt road. The long rolling gate was closed. There was a door of steel bars to the side with a rusted and old intercom on a post. A warning sign was bolted to the bars at eye level:

IS IT WORTH BUCKSHOT UP YOUR ASS?

I pushed the intercom button and spoke in my best harmless, friendly voice. "Hello there, can I come in a retrieve my car, *please*?"

No reply. I looked through the bars for any sign of life. All I could see were rows of smashed cars in stacks. The lock opened with a harsh *clack*.

Entering, I was relieved to see a small gathering of uncrushed cars off to my far right. They were inside a second rectangular fence. I didn't see the Buick, but it might be in a back row. There was a movement to my right, and I froze.

The German Shepard padded up to me, head down, eyes to mine. If dogs could smile, this one was. With a slight wag of its tail.

I put out my hand, fingers tucked safely away.

The dog sniffed and licked my knuckles.

"Nice dog," I said, hoping it was true.

A voice spoke, gruff and sleepy.

"That's cause you ain't done anythin' stupid."

The office door was open and a burly man in a wheelchair was at the top of a ramp. There was something shotgun-long under a blanket in his lap. The office was a singe wide mobile home on a concrete pad.

"Hello," I offered with a smile masking my fear of what was under the blanket.

"What you want?"

"My car was towed. I've come to get it. A Buick Regal."

"That be the one looks like it's already been through the crusher. Only Regal I've got. I take cash or plastic, no personal checks."

"I've got a credit card."

"Come on inside." He rotated the wheelchair and entered the door at his back.

I followed. As did the German Shepard, so far, my new best friend.

"How much do I owe you?" I asked as he rounded his battered steel desk. The air was thick with the smell of fried chicken and a television was running a game show in the lonely family room to the left.

"Three hundred, not counting the city fees."

I had exactly five hundred and sixty-one dollars, not counting the untouchable three hundred thousand.

"How much with the fees included?"

"Four hundred."

"I have that."

"Then make it four-fifty and you get the keys."

The dog idled up to my side. I could hear its breathing and feel its eyes on me. I took out the Hollywood card and *slowly* handed it over the desk.

As the man swiped the card and tapped on the keypad, I looked again to the family room. He had a thing for cowboys. The prints of the walls featured prairie campfires, wagon trains, and gunfights.

"Sign here," he said, tearing the curled receipt from the device.

I scrawled my name with a pen from a peanut can.

"Here's how it works." He put the receipt inside the top drawer. "I'm going to give you the keys to the two padlocks. You bring them back to me after the pen is open. Then you get your car keys. Charlie will go with you."

The man handed me two keys on a ring, and Charlie and I went and unlocked the second fenced yard. I scanned the cars briefly, still not spotting the Buick. I didn't linger, not with the dog poised behind me, my legs looking tasty, I was sure. Charlie followed me back inside the single-wide.

Three minutes later, I found the Buick tucked behind someone's expensive-looking pickup with meaty big tires. Before I climbed in, I looked for my belongings inside on the back seat. Everything was there, under a coating of sand dust dotted by rain drops.

I back the car out and work it around the others out through the gate. Being a somewhat nice guy, I climbed out, rolled the gate closed, and set the padlocks before driving to the exit. A horn crackled, followed by the gate clattering open on steel wheels. I left the stolen bicycle behind for someone else to make use of.

After navigating the badly paved back roads to the coast, I pulled into a sand lot backing a seafood diner. Pulling the briefcase over into the front seat, I unlatched it. Thankfully, there were my belongs, looking untouched. The dead reporter's blood dotted notes were on top. Lifting them away, there was my handgun lying beside Buzz's.

A crashing boom of thunder exploded, scaring me. It sounded like it came from ten feet above the car's roof. I flinched, looking out the missing windshield. A stunning white blast of lighting launched me back hard in the seat. Gun metal gray clouds were rolling in from the ocean.

With the Glock in my lap, I dug my phone from my pocket and opened the search screen. I typed in "Zack" and hit enter.

Exactly one listing came up, and it wasn't a person and the word was spelled differently:

Zack's Boat Launch
211 Cutter Road, West Flagler Beach

Chapter Twenty-Nine

Three Hundred K

Zack's Boat Launch had gone belly up, looking like it died years before. It was beside a strand of tall brush and gray alders. The office and snack bar were shuttered with nailed up plywood that was marked by stapled warning signs. A fish gutting trough ran along the side wall. To the right of the tired office was the boat ramp, a downward slab of concrete. Off to the right, a storm damaged dock tilted out forty feet on the river. A single boat, one of those vacation pontoons, was tied off halfway along. The boat was also leaning, its right-side aluminum float submerged.

The parking lot was empty.

I was seriously early. I could call Lance and tell him thanks, bill me. I could have called my son Bill and asked how he was doing with the sheriff. Instead, I turned the motor off and closed my eyes. No matter the pattering rain coming in through my window and in on the dashboard, I needed to shut down, just for a few. Lack of sleep had me thinking in scattered unconnected snippets, mostly fears of the unknown.

***

I woke to the sound of tires crunching gravel on concrete.

A car pulled in, turned around and backed to the top of the launch ramp to the right, facing me and the Buick.

The car. That car.

Days rolled back.

A dull silver Jaguar in bad need of a car wash.

Maxine.

Her door opened. Before looking to her, I stared in through her windshield, looking for other heads inside. She was alone.

When Maxine climbed out, she had a new look.

New hair. No longer blonde, she was instead a mahogany brunette. She raised her dark glasses, and of all things, smiled to me.

There was her familiar, lovely face. Sparkling, amused blue-gray eyes. Also, a new color.

She was wearing a summer dress of tiny sunflowers on black silk and polished black military boots. I saw the gun at her side, at the ready in her shoulder holster.

She spoke first. Good thing because I sat, staring.

Her other change, her other disguise was talking out of the side of her mouth.

"Inneresting, huh?" she called across in a syrupy Dixie twang.

I opened my door but didn't climb out. My hand went to my lap. *Bring the gun? Hide it how?*

When I stepped out into the rain and winds, I left the gun on the seat, where I could grab it through the missing window if things came to that.

"Where's Kazu?" I called to her.

"Slow down, cowboy, Don'tcha wanna hear how?"

"Not really."

"No, Mister Cameraman? Storytelling is your life work."

"Is he here? Is he okay?" I took out my wallet and removed my Hollywood credit card, my fingers trembling.

"This wasn't a high priority job, at least not at first, 'til we heard the name Kazu. Rex and I had a history with him. The punk didn't steal the Mexican's money, we did. He made a good suspect by runnin' off at the same time. All we had to do was sprinkle a few clues."

Was she stalling? Did she have Kazu? I looked through her windshield again. Nothing.

"Rex and I had a falling out. The hubby wanted to drop the boy and run with the bounty. My plan was to turn you around, after I cleaned out yer rich wife's bank account. Rex didn't agree. No imagination, that one. Not a clue in his pocket."

"Show me Kazu," I demanded, trying to ignore her holstered handgun.

"Rex is now brown bread dead. You saw to that. Was tempted to add to yer bill for the hubby's funeral. Know what I am? Your garden variety dangerous weirdo. Soon to be a rich one."

Would she ever stop blabbing? She took her phone out of her dress pocket and plugged in a credit card reader.

I walked to her, my card extended.

She ran my card.

"Tap in your PIN, if ya would," she purred, turning the phone around.

I entered it with a trembling finger.

She aimed her eyes at me while her phone processed.

I wasn't interested in her hard, steely gaze. I watched the phone in her hand, waiting for a signal that the three hundred thousand had been received. Raindrops spotted the screen. The wet winds were up again.

"Well, ain't that sumthing?" She turned the phone around to me.

I blinked. Had the transfer failed?

"Looks like were done here," she added.

Panic rushed my brain. I took a step back.

Her gun came out in her free hand.

"I can fix this," I promised. "Give me a couple of hours."

"Won't need them. We're good."

"What?" I fought to not stare at the gun aimed at my chest. Her eyes were shining with satisfaction, lowered to the phone.

"Your wifey came through," she said.

I would have felt relief, but for the barrel of the gun pointed at me.

"Then put that down," I said.

"Can't…"

I took a second step back.

"Didja think you and the boy would just walk off along the beach? They want him alive, but understand if…"

There was movement to the right, behind her. My eyes were on the gun, peripheral vision straining.

The rear door of the Jag opened slowly, silently.

She read my eyes, her lips pulling back.

"You've got the money," I pleaded, determined to distract her.

The winds caught the car door. It slammed shut.

She twisted her head fast, getting a quick glimpse.

"No!" she screamed at the side of the Jaguar. "Stop right there!"

I turned to run.

She turned from me and pulled the trigger. The gun *cracked.*

I fell, hitting the ground hard. Spinning around, finding my legs, I ran for the Buick.

The gun fired again.

No impact. I wasn't hit.

Clouting the side of my car, I heard another shot. Ducking, I clenched as her gun fired in three quick loud blasts.

There was a second of silence, except for her screaming. "*Stop! Right! There!*"

I stole a look over the fender.

She was firing across the boat launch.

I reached in, grabbed the Glock, and fingered the safety off.

Swinging around with the gun in my hand, using the fender

as a shield, I aimed it at her.

She fired another round. I hesitated. I had to see.

There he was, bent over, running, hands bound with tape, weaving not slowing. He was on the gravel lot to the side of the ramp, going for the water.

"*Run!*" I screamed at Kazu.

She fired again. I didn't look to him. Instead, I turned to her.

Just like in detective movies, I pulled the trigger three times fast, looked, and fired three more.

"*What the? Nooo!*" Maxine was knocked back, landing on her ass, the back of her head smacking the concrete.

She clambered up, no longer looking to her right, but to me, turning her gun.

I pulled the trigger three more times, trying to aim at her center, the biggest target.

Her knee exploded with a spray of blood. I had no idea where the other bullets went.

Desperate to see if Kazu was okay, I forced myself to keep my eyes and the 9mm aimed at her. I stood from the fender and started forward.

She still clenched her gun in her hand. Blood was running from her center, her stomach and her knee, rain washing it down the ramp in rivulets of warm purple-red.

When I was three steps away, I braved a swipe of my hand cross my face, wiping rain from my eyes.

"Drop that," I insisted, staring at the gun in her hand. "This is done."

She moaned and clenched her eyes tight. "Not quite…"

Her fingers loosened on the grip but didn't let go.

"Not going to ask you to finish me." Her voice was faint, but still cocky. "This ain't no movie."

I said nothing to that.

She gently set her gun on the decline of paving.

"I'll survive." She coughed up red bubbles, her hand gliding from her destroyed knee to her belly.

I stepped to her side and kicked her gun down the ramp, where it splashed into the water between two swollen floating tree limbs and other flotsam, plastic bottles, and rubbish. It was just my nerves that thought the logs leaned away.

Maxine lay back onto her left elbow, eyes clenched, panting in anger and disbelief.

"Be a good guy. Call an ambulance or whoever…" she asked.

I ignored her, turning to the far side of the gravel lot, where I'd last seen Kazu running.

Not seeing his crumbled body, I squeezed my eyes tight with relief.

"Kazu!" I yelled as loud as I could, opening my eyes.

There was movement in the high brush, five feet from the water's edge. Staring through the rain, I tried to make out the shape; desperate to see him, see if he was okay.

Wind swung the vegetation, violently throttling it back and forth.

I lost sight of the shape I knew was my grandson.

"Stop! Your safe now!" I yelled into the wind.

Running, bent forward, Kazu reappeared, spilling, crashing hard onto the rocks at the water line. He didn't slow but found his balance and without hesitation or a single look back, dove into the river.

Chapter Thirty

The Chase

I ran to the spot where Kazu had dove and got one last glimpse of him. He was swimming underwater, twenty feet out, using an aggressive frog kick, his bound hands pointed forward. The rain and wind on the water's surface hid him a second later. It was possible I saw his gray shape turn to his left. I dove in.

Swimming to the spot I had seen him last, the wind and rain were blinding. The last time I had seen him, he was heading south, swimming fast to escape. My clothes weighing me down, he was long gone when I got there. I saw him come up for air, twenty yards to my left. He was swimming parallel to the bank.

"Stop!" I yelled, getting a splash of river water into my mouth for a reply. Coughing it up, I watched his head submerge.

Swimming as fast as possible, I continued the chase. Whitecaps and rain blinding me, I did my best, calling out even when I couldn't see five feet forward. Lightning flashed, blinding me further with a downward blast of hard white light.

When I realized I'd never catch him, I turned to shore.

Climbing out among rocks and brush, I slogged along the bank, needing to see him also climb onto the riverbank.

"Kazu!" I called out and waited.

"Come back! It's safe!"

Nothing carried back to me in the winds and rain. I pressed on.

The going was painfully slow, having to struggle through the dense vegetation and fallen trees. I made another ten yards before I stopped. I was at a wall of stacked coquina stones, four feet tall. As I climbed, I head a new sound.

I froze in place poised on top of the wall. A boat engine was starting, somewhere in the distance. Jumping down, I fought my way to the shore. Standing on a spit of white sand, my eyes followed the revving engine to my left. Seconds later, a shallow fishing skiff headed out to the middle of the wind licked river and turned south. A small, single occupant at the helm.

It had to be him. Where could he go?

***

Back at the boat launch, I started to slog to the Buick when movement on the boat ramp stopped me short. Wiping rain from my face, I stared, jaw dropped.

In the waters at the base of the ramp, the two logs I'd seen before were moving, climbing, swaying; the alligator on the left had its snout raised, its jaws yawed open.

Seeing my Glock laying a few feet above where Maxine lay, I didn't move until my next step came to me. Ignoring her silent dying gaze, I eased my gun into her hand and pressed her finger on the trigger. Then I walked away from her, back up the ramp. Later, I would struggle with that decision.

Wounded, bloodied Maxine screamed. One last time.

***

I crossed to her Jaguar and opened the rear door. On the floorboard was a roll of duct tape and Kazu's backpack. I zipped it open. There was his black and gold Pirates' baseball cap on top of a ziplocked bag of his drawings, his "image-novels," as Feeb had described them. I dug deeper, fingers clawing the canvas bottom. My hand came away with a battered boy's wallet. It had not been opened in years; I pried the faux leather apart. It was empty except for an aged, yellowed card. There was printing across the top.

Hutchinson County, Kansas
Library Membership

Below was Kazu's much younger signature above his typed name.

With the card back in the wallet and the wallet inside the backpack along with his hat, I left it in the car, leaving the door open. Sliding his plastic covered drawings inside my shirt, I headed for my car. I was leaving the scene of a vicious alligator attack that had claimed two lives.

Chapter Thirty-One

WESH

What was I becoming? What had I become?

It came to me, direct and true.

Like my grandson, I was cornered and saw no other options. I was up against his similar choices.

Like that fine twelve-year-old boy, I was a killer.

Aimlessly driving the backroads in the general direction of the coast, each quarter mile from Zack's Boat Launch brought no relief. Kazu was out there somewhere, navigating the white capped river. He was still on the run, surely frightened and alone. Nowhere to go, nowhere to hide, no idea that Maxine had been stopped for good.

Driving in the rain without a windshield was madness. I could barely see parked cars and stops signs, squinting into the gray day, the headlights not helping at all. Worse than the rains, I was at a loss as to where to search next.

Finding myself at a stop before north and south running A1A, I looked in both directions.

"Next?" was my simpleton's question. The highway had nothing to say to that.

I turned right, to the south, for no good reason except that was the direction Kazu had been heading last. The storm out over the Atlantic had a curious trailing form of clouds to the south. An extended gray arm above the white caps. Like a tattered sleeve, a row of dangling, falling tendrils of rain were one beside the other. Was that a new kind of storm approaching?

Leaving Flagler Beach, I drove along the coast, the wild lands to my right. Entering Ormond Beach, I slowed with the start of condos, beach-facing restaurants, and cheap motels. With no new ideas coming, I decided I need to regroup, however brief.

According to my scattered mind, there was one hundred eleven dollars left on the Hollywood card. I hit a fast-food drive thru and a few miles farther saw a sign for a $45 per night motel rooms.

After another white bag dinner at the table under the window, I desperately needed just an hour of sleep after a long shower. Pulling off my soaked dank clothes and shoes, I adjusted the water's temperature to warm, near hot, and stepped in.

Sitting on the shower floor, I formed a viewfinder with my thumbs and fingers. My mind wanted to imagine the gruesome final moments of Maxine feeding the alligators. I fought that off by giving it a black and white filter and moving it to the far bottom right of the composition. What came next was the back of Kazu's head as he surfaced for air on the river. A disturbing spray of blood followed, drops running down the screen. I mentally wiped that nightmare away, smearing the lens.

"Where would Kazu run to?" I asked the viewfinder. "Alone in that stolen boat."

That April woman's garage?

The dance house as Feeb called it?

Then there it was, tinted in smudged red.

The third and strongest image. The screen went black and theatrically dramatic typing crossed.

TO HIS GIRLFRIEND'S SIDE,
THE BRAVE AND RESOURCEFUL FEEB.

Leaving the shower, I took my phone from my soaked pants and called my son, Bill.

"Hello, Dad." His voice was strained and formal, a sure sign of stress.

"You doing okay?" I asked.

"Sure. Best I can with all this."

"Yes. All this. Where are you?"

"Just left the sheriff's department. They're a fine bunch. I have to leave the room when they talk, but I think they have some ideas, some leads."

"That's encouraging. Where are you headed?"

"Dad? I've no idea except not returning to the hotel. I climb the walls there."

"I get that," I glanced at my own dismal room, which was somehow accusing me. *Get out there. Do something.*

"I didn't mention Kazu's past like you asked. They didn't ask," he said. "They are more focused on his past few days. They're a bit scattered. That murder on the bridge has them light staffed."

"Good. Let them do all they can to find him. His past life doesn't matter. Any idea where they're searching."

"I get concerned looks and sincere pats on the shoulder. Other than that, they're keeping it to themselves."

"I've got an idea," I said. "Two actually."

"Really? How can I help?"

"There are two places he's sometimes stayed."

"Where? I'll go right away."

I gave him the location of April's garage and Maison de Danse.

"I'll hit the garage first, then the other place," Bill said. "Repeatedly. Forever, until he shows."

"Good. Yes. Even if it doesn't play out."

"It's something and better that sitting around inside a saltine box. Want to come along with me?"

"Can't. There's someone I need to track down."

"Who?"

"One of his street friends if I can find her."

"Let me know how it goes."

"You do the same."

The call ended. I pulled on dry cloths and left the motel.

***

There was no sign of her at the 7-Eleven. Not a hint of Feeb or her friends along the rain-swept streets or along A1A with its row of restaurants, gift shops, and real estate offices. I turned to the back streets. The town was laid out in a grid of bungalows and cottages, abruptly interrupted here and there by new, stately, mini mansions. I worked the grid north to south and back again. Nighttime came, and I continued.

Two hours later, I gave up on the search. The houses were dark, and the streets abandoned. I hadn't seen as much as a glimpse of Feeb or any other kids seeking shelter from the storm.

Back inside my motel room, I turned on the television. After a scroll, I found WESH, channel 2, with a news broadcast running.

A red banner lay across the bottom of the screen with BREAKING NEWS. Above it stood a newscaster out in the rain, microphone to her lips.

"Details are sketchy, but here's what I've learned so far…"

Behind her, fifteen yards back, was Zack's Boat Launch, complete with drooping yellow crime scene tape. Several officers were walking fast and there were three cruisers with their red and blues sweeping.

"At least one death, possibly two," the broadcaster continued, looking saddened and struggling and somewhat like a drenched puppy, wet tangles of hair trying to hide her lovely, striking face. When she turned to her right, the camera panned with her.

"It's suspected that the driver of the Jaguar was one of the victims. As you can see, the car is being searched carefully. Evidence on the boat ramp suggest a horrible death of one, possibly two victims…" Pausing for dramatic effect, she added, "There are clear indications of an alligator attack."

I turned off the television. They would find Kazu's wallet and that's all that mattered.

Heading back out into the night, I would search for the girl until dawn if need be. Even if futile, my spirits were lifted by looking for Feeb. As soon as they opened Kazu's wallet, they would know the name of at least one of the deceased and might end their hunt for him.

Chapter Thirty-Two

Daytona News-Journal

Bill was out searching for his son all night as well. Driving back and forth between April's garage and the Maison de Danse compound, he texted me each time he arrived at one of the places. He was watching one of the residences for a half hour before driving to the other. At two in the morning, he sent:

> Back at April's. All lights out. Snuck in and knocked on the garage door. Nothing. Tried the woman's back door. The cameras came on, but no one answered.

> You're doing fine, I encouraged him.

I was down on the beach, north of the Flagler pier, walking to the camp in the tall grass the kids had shared with me. A high tide had washed out their small clearing, filling their fire pit, which was then a bowl of sand. The only sign of them was that old beach umbrella Feeb sometimes carried, laying in the grass at the back of their abandoned camp.

Back in the Buick, I continued my slow drive along the back streets of the beach town.

My last sighting of Kazu came to me without the need of a viewfinder. I texted Bill.

He has a boat. A fishing skiff. I heard there's a dock at the compound.

I'll search for it, he replied immediately

I wished that had come to me sooner. Feeb had told me about the dock, and I had failed to walk it.

Exhausted and eyes stinging from lack of sleep, I stopped my search for Feeb one time, entering an all-night CircleK gas station for a large cup of bold and bitter coffee. Back to the streets and the search, I hoped the caffeine would sharpen me.

Sometime later, Bill texted again.

Found the dock across the street from the compound. Empty.

At four-thirty that morning, I must have nodded off, the coffee failing me. The Buick shuddered and my eyes went wide. I had run up on a sidewalk.

Steering back into the street, I took two strong pulls of the coffee. My phone vibrated on the dash.

Dad? I'll keep at this forever, but we're no closer to him. The sun will be up soon. You okay with me checking in with the sheriffs? Maybe they have something else I can do to help?

He was right. No question. I replied:

I agree. We've hit it hard but got nowhere. If you can, please don't mention me.

I gave the streets another hour before pulling into the 7-Eleven parking lot. I poured the CircleK coffee on the pavement and headed inside to buy one of those little bottles of five-hour energy. Selecting the Blue Raspberry flavor, Feeb's favorite, I asked the salesclerk, "Seen any of those kids that always hang around here?"

He shook his head, not saying a word, eyeing me like a probable pedophile. The glass door opened, followed by a wordless *thump*. The morning edition of the *Daytona Beach News-Journal* had been delivered.

"One second," I told the clerk, who had his hand out for my credit card. I crossed to the news rack and read the headline over the fold. I reread the loud banner twice, a hot sweat pouring from my skin, my face flushing with fear.

Chapter Thirty-Three

Blue and Red

TWO LOCAL MURDERS LINKED?

Under the headline were two color photos, side by side, both from crime scenes. The first image was of the blood and evidence markers on the grating of the drawbridge with Rex's U-Haul van in the background.

The second large photograph was from Zack's Boat launch, where an evidence technician knelt before the open door of the Jaguar.

By Hank Fernandez
Early Edition

FLAGLER BEACH – The two cruel and vicious murders in our otherwise quiet and safe community have shocked local residences. Occurring just days apart, the crimes were first considered separate events until both victims were identified. The crucial link is their shared last names. Rex and Maxine Thurges, both 39, from Brownsville, Texas.

Both murders were marked by cold blooded cruelty, suggesting a professional killer's involvement.

Mr. Thurges was run over at least three times after failing to stop the murderer by firing his handgun several times.

If possible, what occurred at the boat lunch was worse. Mrs. Thurges was first wounded by gunfire before being dragged down the boat ramp in the jaws of one or more alligators.

Was there a third victim? The task force isn't saying, but as reported before, a search of Mrs. Thurges automobile was conducted, and a child's backpack was seen being placed in an evidence bag.

Were the Thurges' involved in foul play at the time of their deaths? The Thurges jointly owned a Brownsville detective agency, specializing in what their website advertises as, "Professional Felon Apprehension on both sides of the border and bounty services throughout middle America and the East Coast."

In 2012, Rex Thurges pleaded guilty to charges of second-degree assault and one count of attempted extortion in the shooting of David Bodisher in the Chester Gorge parking lot on April 3, 2011, according to court records.

Mr. Thurges was originally charged with attempted murder for the shooting, which authorities said was part of an effort by Mr. Thurges to apprehend Bodisher on a Federal warrant.

Mr. Thurges was sentenced to one to three years in state prison as part of a plea agreement reached in the case, according to court records. He was also discharged from the US Marshals service.

Mrs. Maxine Thurges is not known to have a criminal record.

The Flagler Beach Police Department and Volusia County Sheriff's Department are cooperating on the investigation, having set up a temporary field office at the scene of second murder, in the parking lot of Zack's Boat Launch, long out of business.

The task force is aggressively pursuing all leads to quickly identify and apprehend the suspected killer.

Anyone with information about these two cases is urged to call the hotline at (386) 248-1777 or KGlaesel@vcso.us

I put the newspaper back in the rack and climbed into the Buick, the car itself the strongest link between me at the killings. Steering from the parking lot, I looked to the distant west. The clouds were parting slowly, offering a promise of an improvement in the weather, the opening in the sky a summer tropical blue. Driving slow and cautious, I stayed to the back streets.

Two miles up along the river road, a siren bleeped in the early morning air, followed by swirling red and blue lights in my side mirrors.

"No, no, you can't," I cursed, hands clenching the wheel. I slowed up but didn't stop. There on the passenger seat was my briefcase. Best I could remember, Buzz Guzman's 9mm was still inside, along with the very suspicious files. A quick glance back showed me the officer's head with a microphone in hand.

I turned on the blinkers. Never a thought of trying to run. My mind raced with my only other option; a story of innocence, including my best befuddled tourist imitation.

Stopping in front of a pale green cottage with beachy décor, I put the Buick in park, but left the motor running. During the next painfully creeping few minutes, I got the registration from the glove box and my license from my wallet, constantly glancing into the side mirror. If that door swung open fast, I knew I'd see an officer with gun drawn. So far, all I could see was a conversation being conducted through the microphone. Was backup being called in? Was I about to be swarmed and handcuffed and led away?

So far, I didn't hear approaching sirens. Two more minutes ticked away, one second after another. *Bought the car in a bar last night. I shouldn't drink. How is your morning, officer?* There was my first line if I was given the opportunity.

The car door in the side mirror opened. It had a sheriff's department emblem. The officer was moving slow. Almost casually. I stared, breathe clenched. So far, no gun out. With the registration card and my license in my trembling hand, I worked the other mirrors, wishing the rearview hadn't disappeared with the windshield. The officer rounded slowly to the passenger side window.

"Good morning, sir," she said.

I was washed with a cleansing cold with the first friendly words.

"Yes, it is," I said.

"License and registration, please," she asked, voice firm, but polite.

I handed them over. Before she carried them back to her cruiser, I read the brass nametag on her uniform—Deputy Janelle Dicks.

My right-side mirror showed her climbing inside and leaning to her right, to a dash mounted computer. She was also taking a call from the microphone on her shoulder. When her door reopened, she was moving briskly but still no gun drawn. In fact, she was looking in my direction with a terse smile.

I leaned to the passenger window and she handed me my papers.

"Mr. Danser, there are at least seven serious operational issues with your vehicle. I want those taken care of immediately. If this rental is seen again without repairs, you are going to have a handful of fix it tickets. Do you understand?"

"Yes. Of course. I'll take care of them today. I promise."

"See to it. I'm giving you walk this morning. There are other serious fish frying right now."

"Thank you," I said, relieved that the Buick had somehow not yet been linked to either of the two murders. The *yet* was huge. I had an idea.

"Is it possible," I asked, forcing a smile, "I could have one of your cards? New to town, it would a comfort to have a contact in the sheriff's department."

"Sure." She quickly took out a black card holder and handed me one. "Gotta run," she added, leaving me sitting there while she jogged to her car.

When, not *if*, my car was linked to the double killings, it might help to know a familiar face and name to tell some version of my story to.

***

Don't know that I breathed much until the battered and suspect Buick was hidden behind a abandoned grocery store. Suitcase in one hand, briefcase in the other, I headed away fast, but not running suspiciously. I felt the rising heat of the day and with it an oppressive humidity that dampened my face and shirt.

Two residential blocks along, my phone buzzed.

"You've got to wait a few," I spoke to whoever was calling. At least until I found my hotel and was inside my room.

Suitcase dropped and the briefcase on the table, I dug out my phone.

It only took a few seconds to recognize the number from the voicemail. I had to sit down, my heart was racing in my chest, my pulse over the top. Desperately wanting a deep drink of water, I didn't leave the table. Instead, I hit play.

A moment of static. No voice. No words. I stared at the little screen for a minute, willing to phone to ring again. Another minute slipped by. Then three more.

"Call me back!" I shouted.

A hundred and twenty dragging seconds passed.

In a fright, I looked at the battery life. One-third remaining.

A bead of sweat ran down my nose. If I had turned, I would have seen the walls of the motel room falling away, leaving nothing but me and the cellphone.

Another minute passed.

The phone quivered in both my unsteady hands and its incoming call display glowed. I hit answer before the first ring had a chance to finish.

Chapter Thirty-Four

The call

"Grandpa?"

Kazu's child voice had changed. There was a sandpaper deepening from nearly being a teen.

"Can you help me?"

Chapter Thirty-Five

Third Victim

"Where are you?" I asked my grandson. "I'm coming. You're safe now. Just tell me where."

"I'm safe for now, but there's this woman hunting me."

That was Maxine, of course.

"She's been stopped." I said no more.

"How do you know? Are you sure?"

"Trust me on that one. Where are you?"

"My friend Ben's shop. He let Feeb and I sleep in the storeroom."

"What store? I'll come get you."

"Nerdz, but I'm leaving. His wife is pissed."

"Wait outside. I'm on my way."

"I can't. There are cops everywhere. Grandpa? I'm wanted for doing a bunch of bad stuff."

"I know. And it's in the past. Besides, I think I've dusted your trail."

There was a pause, followed by Kazu saying, "Let's meet at the farmer's market. I'll be there in an hour."

"Here in Flagler?"

"Yes. Second Street right off the beach. There'll be a crowd, which is safer for me."

"One hour. Got it. I'll be there."

A woman's tired and frustrated voice was berating someone in the background.

Kazu ended the call with, "Gotta run."

***

I called Bill.

"Drop everything," I told him as soon as he picked up. "Get to Flagler Beach. The farmer's market."

"Of course. What's up?"

"We found him!" I couldn't contain myself, those three words tasting amazingly sweet. They must have sounded the same. There was a silence between us as it sank in.

Bill gasped and coughed.

I closed my eyes, letting him have as long as he needed.

"Dad?" he broke the spell. Measuring out in a hoarse voice, he asked, "You have him?"

"Not yet. But he'll be there within the hour."

"How? No, that can wait. Where's this farmer's market?"

"Kazu told me it's on Second Street by the beach."

"You spoke to him?"

"Briefly, yes. He sounds good. Scared, but okay."

Car keys jingled on Bill's end of the call.

"On my way," he breathed. "One other thing, first."

"Quickly, sure," I said.

"The sheriff just called me a few minutes ago. Wants me to come in. Said it's urgent."

"What for?" I was confused and needed to know what they were up to. What did they want from him? Urgently?

"They asked if I was aware of your being in the area," Bill sounded equally confused. "I stalled by asking what's up?"

"And they said?"

"A witness called the hotline this morning. She said she saw your car near that boat ramp killing and called the number in the newspaper. Dad, what's going on? Where you there?"

What to share? What to say? I didn't answer.

"Dad?"

"I'm here." Guilty and the net closing in.

"Also told me you were pulled over this morning, but you slipped away. Someone's in hot water for that."

They were connecting the dots quickly.

"Dad, were you somehow involved in the stuff in the papers?"

I hesitated, turning away. Staring at the television on top of the dresser, I went with as much truth as I saw was safe to share.

"I was there," I admitted. "For good reason."

"Okay," my son sounded sad. "Okay," he repeated. "Let's find Kazu. Sort everything else out later."

Before I could agree, he ended the call.

***

I had forty-five minutes to get to the farmer's market, just a few blocks away. I needed to get there early. But I also needed to know *if* I could get there.

I turned on the television.

WESH, Channel 2 was featuring the latest on the double homicides. Fresh video from the second crime scene was swept from the screen, replaced by several police and sheriffs in front of a dais with a cluster of microphones. Glaring across the bottom of the screen was:

BREAKING NEWS: SUSPECT IDENTIFIED:
THIRD VICTIM IDENTIFIED.

"A third victim has been identified by evidence at the scene of the boat launch murder. A child, we regret to say. We won't be releasing his name until notification of kin."

A flurry of shouting from the gathered press followed. The uniformed spokesman quieted them by patting his hands down in the air.

"We've also learned that a witness has identified a vehicle likely driven by the assailant. We have all joint resources searching for the vehicle. In a moment, we'll be posting its description. If anyone has seen this car, please call our hotline immediately."

Questions were shouted by the reporters. The officer crossed his arms and waited until that ended a half-minute later.

"At this time, we're releasing the following on Mr. and Mrs. Thurges, the other two victims. Originally from Brownsville, Texas, we've learned that the couple was pursing an unidentified criminal here in Volusia County. The Thurges are the proprietors of a detective agency that also had its hands in bounty hunting, a description long out of favor. A team of investigators are flying to Brownsville as I speak. The authorities there have been notified and have search warrants in hand."

"Who were they hunting for?" a female reported pressed as the spokesman took a breath.

"All in good time. You have my word," he said. Looking to one of his fellow officers, he asked, "Noon?"

The uniformed woman nodded.

"That's all for now," The spokesman told the press and the cameras. "Please join us at twelve o'clock for another briefing. We will be taking questions at that time."

He stepped back and away as questions were called out. The live feed from the press conference ended, replaced by a stock photograph of a Buick Regal. I turned the television off as the hotline number appeared in the lower red banner.

I had to put all that aside. I knew I would be in their hands soon. I left the motel room and started walking up the street, head down, listening for running footsteps, shouts or sirens.

They could have me. Just not yet.

Chapter Thirty-Six

Farmer's Market

The farmer's market was on a sand lot one block in from the coast. Above, the sky was divided, menacing gray overhead and tropical blue to the west. There were maybe seventy-five people, including the vendors, the warm, gentle falling rain not keeping them away. Many of the shoppers pulled their weekly grocery carts, chatting with the merchants. Others were dressed for vacation, milling table to table with cups of coffee. A young couple was rolling a stroller with a dog inside.

Entering from the west side, sun on my back, I waded in, my eyes scanning, searching desperately for Kazu.

"Excuse me." I squeezed past an elderly couple, both with full shopping bag in their arms, adding the "Sorry" I didn't feel.

I was looking at each face long enough to discard them, focusing on shorter people. I went up the first aisle of wood tables with colorful produce: fresh vegetables and fruit. One vendor was selling jars of honey and maple syrup. Another offered handmade soap and shampoo. A knife sharpening vendor was working from the rear of his pickup.

No sign of Kazu.

I rounded the last table and hurried through the crowd, face after face, nudging, bumping shoulders and tossing out apologies. Halfway up the middle aisle, I picked out Feeb's friend, Slurp. He was alone, probably nicking fruit into the backpack hanging at his side. Instead of stopping to question him, I wiped warm rain drops from my face to see better.

Where was he?

Something hold him up?

I pushed that aside, working my way to the end of the row of tables.

I looked to the four corners of the sand lot before entering the last row. New arrivals were strolling in, no youths, no hint of my grandson.

"Dad!" Bill's voice called.

I turned around. He was crossing the street from the north at a run. Wadding through the shoppers, he was wild-eyed; a beautiful, foolish grin of hope on his face.

"Any sign of him?" he shouted.

I shook my head, calling back, "Keep trying," like there was anything else he might do.

While he hurried up the middle aisle, I made my way to the end of the last row, frustrated, but determined. I did a three-sixty, eyes straining. Bill was calling his son's name.

"Kazu! Kazu!"

I saw Feeb first, turning the corner of a shop across Second Street. She was mincing her steps, walking slow, hesitantly, eyes sweeping side to side. Her arm was stretched backward. Sudden warm sunlight filled the air at my back as the rain continued to fall a few feet in front of me. She was whispering over her shoulder.

A second later, Kazu appeared, holding her hand.

His eyes were scanning back and forth, his expression wary and suspicious. He was in black shorts and shirt and black work boots. Stepping into the street, he moved like a cat, not at all trusting a bowl of fresh milk. To anyone else, he looked like another Florida street urchin.

"Kazu!" Billed yelled again.

Kazu flinched before turning to the sound of his father's voice.

Kazu searched, turning his head left to right.

To my left, Bill was parting the crowd at a run.

"Is that really you?" my son yelled.

Kazu turned his eyes. And froze.

There was his dad, running to him, chanting, "It's you! It's you!"

Feeb gently let go of Kazu's hand and spoke to his ear.

He turned to her, and I saw him smile. A familiar expression, but from so many years before.

He jogged forward, eyes no longer worried with anything; aimed solely at his father's brilliantly happy face.

Father and son embraced in the middle of the street, clenching each other, swaying.

Both leaned back and they studied each other, eye to eye. Bill was chanting, "You! It's you!" Kazu was bobbing his head, agreeing, not speaking.

Before starting to them, my hands rose, and my fingers instinctively formed a viewfinder. No collage, no puzzle. In the only way I knew how, I captured the memory to archive forever. It was pure cinema of love. I blinked my eyes, which were filling, saying over my shoulder, "Swelling violins soundtrack, please."

Feeb joined them. Watching, smiling, approaching tentatively, like not wanting to intrude.

My son's arm went around her shoulder, and he pulled her close as well.

Holding Kazu tight to his chest, Bill beckoned to me over his son's shoulder.

"Put that thing down, Dad." He meant the silly viewfinder.

I did. And entered the street to join their delightful reunion.

A hand clenched my shoulder. Another clamped my elbow,

locking on tight, twisting my arm backward.

"Hands behind your back." I recognized the officer's voice. It was Deputy Janelle Dicks, who had kindly not written the many fix-it tickets earlier that morning.

I complied.

Chapter Thirty-Seven

Solitary

Sneaking one last look over my shoulder, there was Kazu in the arms of his dad and girlfriend. I was escorted up Second Street into brilliant sunlight under the warm blue sky. Placed inside the second of two sheriff cruisers parked one block up, I was read my Miranda's by Deputy Janelle Dicks.

We rode in silence to the sheriff's station. I was grateful for the quiet. I had a story to pull together—thankfully, most of it would be the truth. Truth, except for one part; the most important. Kazu was free. All I had to do was keep him dead to all the world.

After being booked and fingerprinted, I was led to a holding cell to await the arrival of investigators. As the steel door was about to shut, Deputy Janelle Dicks spoke to me, her voice caring and almost kind.

"You won't look too bad in orange."

***

Without a clock, my guess is that I sat in the solitary cell for three to four hours.

When the heavy lock clicked and the door opened, I assumed it was finally time for the authorities to start asking their questions. After being cuffed again, I was led up the hall to an interview room.

Seated at the table with me was Chief Deputy Dan Mills and a detective from the Flagler Beach Police Department. Chief Deputy Mills did all the talking, starting out pleasantly.

"Mr. Danser, sorry for the delay. We had a squabble over turf with the Flagler Police Department. All sorted out now," he nodded to the detective at his side.

"First thing first. Willing to talk with us?"

It was ask for a lawyer time.

"Let's see how it goes," I answered.

"Good, yes. Let's chat and see where we get."

"What have I been charged with?"

"Nothing yet. The D.A. is on his way."

"Murder by Buick," the police detective spoke for the first and last time.

It was almost funny. Deputy Ron Mills looked at him like he was from another planet and continued.

"Tell me your story. Start from the beginning. What brought you to sunny Florida?"

"My grandson, Kazu Danser," I said. "He called me out of the blue a few days ago. Needed my help."

"He was your grandson? My condolences."

With that said, I felt an immense relief. I took them back to my arrival in Daytona, no mention of my time at the Mexican border, not a word about my good friend, Buzz Guzman, the private investigator. Not a peep about Rhonda's assistance. What they heard was the story of a confused and determined grandpa looking for his runaway grandson.

Twenty minutes later, we were at the drawbridge part of the story.

"The man had my number, somehow. Said he had Kazu.

Wanted money in exchange for his freedom. Something went wrong. I don't know what. He started firing a gun at me. There was nothing I could do but use me car… to stop him."

"He was alone? Did you see your grandson?"

"We were both alone. No sign of Kazu."

"You were alone?" The deputy looked puzzled. He opened the folder he had carried into the room.

"Do you know the name Buzz Guzman?"

"No. Who is he?"

"Let move on. Were you at Zack's Boat Launch the day of a second murder and… the loss of your grandson?"

"I would give my life to go back in time and be there. I might have been able to save him before…" no need to mention Kazu's gruesome death in the jaws of an alligator.

"We have a witness placing your car nearby on that day."

"Don't know what to say to that except I was driving everywhere. Day and night, searching for him."

"To clarify, were you there when Mrs. Thurges… and Kazu… met their unfortunate deaths?"

"No."

Best I could tell, I had dusted the trails of my involvement in the deaths of the two bounty hunters. That said, it was probably time to lawyer up. I was about to ask to make a phone call when Deputy Mills closed his folder and leaned back in his chair.

"I think we're good for now. Least until the D.A. gets here. You're to be remanded until we meet and go over your story and the case files."

Five minutes later, I was back in my solitary cell. I asked to place a call. There was a payphone in another high security room with a worn-out phone book dangling on a chain. I didn't look up attorneys. Even if I wanted to, my estimate was that I had seventeen dollars available on my credit card. I had exactly one number memorized.

I called Rhonda.

Chapter Thirty-Eight

"Death Can Be Murder"

The wheels of the criminal justice system turn slow as they should; thoroughness being critical in the pursuit of the truth. I was in my cell for three long days of boredom, interrupted by daily questioning with Chief Deputy Mills and others as well as conferences with the attorney Rhonda hired for me: my ninety-pound land shark as I came to think of her.

The lawyer's name was Sandra Colson. She always appeared in a black business suit, black attaché in hand, white blouse, and a clenched smile that didn't show in her eyes. Her mind was elsewhere, working lightning fast. I learned quickly that there was nothing casual or beach-like about "Sandy" as she insisted I call her when we first met.

During the first conference, I told Sandy the story exactly as shared with the authorities.

We met again the next day. She sat across from me and looked me straight in the eyes.

"It is a grievous misunderstanding. They're coming around to that. The D.A.'s ninety-five percent there. I'll be nailing down the five percent before he and I meet at six tonight."

"Can you get me bailed out?" I asked.

"We're not asking for bail. Screw that. I'm getting you released *by their order*. I want you out of here all crisp and clean and declared innocent."

"You're brilliant at this, aren't you?"

"Brilliant and expensive. The best are."

"Speaking of you fee. I need to work on that with my friend Rhonda."

"Already spoke to her." She took a new folder from her attaché and set it on the table with a pen.

"The divorce docs," I said, recognizing them.

"That they are."

I took up the pen and opened the folder. Signing my name was inevitable. I had stalled for months on end. A few pen strokes and Pauline would be free to enjoy another life. I wanted that for her, no question, no hesitation. We had tried and loved each other famously. We had weathered all the good and the bad and some of the best times possible. But now that ship was under tattered sails and was rudderless and floundering.

"I've got a better idea." I set the pen down.

"Your call. There's absolutely no push for payment. My priority is getting you out of here, cleared and free."

We spent fifteen minutes discussing what was likely to be happening over the next twenty-four hours, Sandy doing most of the talking, as was best. When she left, the divorce paperwork went with her.

Why hadn't I signed? I clearly knew I was going to. The problem was, I wasn't going to end my marriage for quick money. Simple as that.

***

I walked from the sheriff's department in my raggedy street clothes, Sandy at my side. The sunlight was blinding and perfect. There were two reporters watching on. Sandy turned her head, but not her body, aiming the eyes of a carnivore at them. Not a word was exchanged. We walked through the midday heat to the parking lot.

Sandy stopped and held out her hand.

"I'm confident your belonging's will be released to you no later than tomorrow morning."

"That'll be good." I shook her small hand.

"I'm sorry about the loss of your grandson. I hope you can move on with your life."

"That's the plan," I replied. "Thank you for everything."

She gave me a brief, stilted hug.

"Time will help," she suggested.

"Yes." I watched her get into her car and drive away.

Bill was waiting for me, leaning against the side of his rental car, watching on, grinning.

"Hey there," he greeted me, his voice thick, his eyes tired and pleased.

Stepping into his open arms, I told him, "Thank you for picking me up."

"Get in," he leaned back. "Let's never see this place again."

"Agreed." I circled to the passenger side.

"Where would you like to go first?" He started the car.

Looking at the plastic evidence bag I had carried from the jail, there was my phone and wallet received while being processed out.

"Dad?" Bill asked.

"Sorry. A shower and a bed."

"You've got it. I'll get you a room where I'm staying."

He steered the streets to the right turn onto southbound A1A.

"Bill?"

"Yes?"

"Where's Kazu?"

"With him mom. I put him on a flight two days ago. Feeb

went with him. She doesn't have parents to ask."

And so there it was. The rare, happy ending. Kazu was free. Safe and home again.

I looked straight up, right through the roof of the car. Relief filled my heart. Tears filled my eyes.

"Thank you," I whispered to my wondrous, guiding stars.

I reached over and took Bill's hand.

"Dad, you okay?" he asked.

"I am now."

***

"Pull in here, please," I asked Bill as we came up on a CircleK mini mart. "I'll just be a minute." He pulled in and I went inside the store alone. I looked to the newspaper rack and passed. The headline told me all I needed to know:

DOUBLE HOMICIDE: SUSPECT RELEASED

At the Holiday Inn, Bill rented me a room down the hall from his. We agreed to have dinner later that night and parted with room keys in hand.

After those days in the concrete shoebox, the clean room and its décor was a welcome sight. I didn't linger but went to the bathroom. After putting my dead phone on its charger, I started the shower. Taking my time, I used up the little bottles of bath gel and shampoo. One of the wonders of hotels is the endless supply of warm water. I needed the time. I had to wash away the question that had haunted me since my arrest.

While hunting for Kazu, three people had died. Buzz Guzman and Rex and Maxine Thurges. Rhonda had also been dragged through hell at my doing.

No viewfinder was needed. Their faces were with me, watching on as I struggled with the deadly consequences of my hunt for Kazu.

Does this ending—Kazu's freedom—justify all that I had done? I asked myself for the hundredth time.

No answer came. Only two words *could* allow me to move on, to accept.

"With time?" I whispered.

"Help me so I can be good with this someday," I asked the swirling mist above my head.

***

With my phone charged, I sat on the foot of the bed. Sleep in a clean large bed was pulling at me and I knew I would cave soon, but first I had to tie some things up.

"Hey ya, Pie," Rhonda answered halfway through the first ring. "Lawyer told me you're a free man. Welcome back."

"Thank you. How are you doing?"

"Ducky. No need to ask how you're doing, after getting out of handcuffs."

"Right. And thank you again. For everything."

"Keep saying nice things. Keep me buttered up."

"Gladly," I said and paused.

"And?" Rhonda read the hesitation.

"The divorce papers."

"And?"

"Before I sign, can you add an addendum to them?"

"On it. Whatcha want to add?"

"I'm refusing all settlement monies."

"Go you! Give me a fax number and I'll send the revision over."

I read her the number off the courtesy card on the night table.

"Check the front desk in about a half hour," she said. "Interesting decision and welcome to poverty."

We both grinned at that—I could hear hers.

"Another favor?" I asked.

"Shoot."

I blanched at that and said, "I want to sell the dealership."

"Okay. Why?"

"I need to repay the loan from Pauline."

"The three hundred thousand? Use the dealership's credit line, boy-o."

I hadn't thought of that. I didn't know it had one.

"I can draw up the bank papers," she offered. "Probably get you funded in a week or two."

Looking at the door to the room, I shook my head. It came to me quick and sure. I was not turning around.

"Let's sell it, instead," I said.

"Aren't we getting all decisive?"

We shared another silent grin.

"Pie? I've been talking to Pauline. Well, not talking, but I'm replying to her telegrams. She is over the top with the news of Kazu's return."

"Yes. You and I…" I got out, closing my eyes.

"We did good. A bit messy, but…" She paused, too. When she continued, her voice was soggy with emotion.

"That amazing boy is back on the farm. Returned to his ma and pa and baby brother."

"Yes. And Roadkill."

"Excuse me, but huh?"

"A dog."

"Of course. Anything else you need me to look into?"

"Yes. Book yourself that champagne cruise. My treat."

"I will. *After* you're solvent."

"Thank you."

"Will you stop with those? I gotta run, fires to start, fires to put out."

***

The next day, after much paperwork and signatures, I was handed the keys to my battered Buick and drove away, my belongings resting on the back seat. Overnight, Rhonda had worked her persuasive magic and unfroze my other two bank cards. With a little money to burn, I called Bill and we agreed to meet at the Oceanside restaurant in Flagler Beach for lunch.

We took a table up on the top deck, where we could enjoy a view of the blue Atlantic.

"What time's your flight?" I asked Bill after we had ordered.

"Not until five. Plenty of time," Bill looked around at the happy diners at the other tables, all tan and delighted with the warm and sunny day.

"Think of it, Dad. By this evening, I'll be home. Ali. Dan the Baby. And Kazu. I can't wait. Why don't you come with me?"

Two glasses of water appeared on the table, giving me the pause I needed.

"I will come soon. Not just yet," I said. "You fly home and celebrate."

"That's a given, but I'd love to have you there for that."

"Soon as I take care of a few things, I'll be there. That's a promise."

We clicked our water glasses.

Lunch was served. After the waiter left, Bill said, "Did you know that there's a clan of Dansers down here? You could look them up if you're sticking around. I met our Aunt Izzy, not sure how distantly removed."

I remembered. The female voice behind the locked gate of the Maison de Danse compound.

"She's certainly one of us." Bill smiled while setting his fork down. "A *strange* duck, but she warmed a little when I told her I was a Danser."

"Interesting. Did you get inside the place? I had no luck with her."

"I wish. She's very protective of her privacy. My *mon refuge de clairs et somber*, she said. Sounded French. I could hear loud rock music coming from far back. Anyway, she wished me well and told me, 'Don't come back here.' Then she faded in the distance, singing."

"It's interesting, but I'm done with puzzles for a while."

"Same."

When the bill came, I paid it and we took the stairs down to the parking lot.

"Take care, Dad," he told me. "I love you. Come to the farm soon as you can."

"Good as done. I love you, too."

We embraced and I stood still until his car rolled out onto northbound A1A.

***

Taking out my car keys, I walked to the sorry looking Buick—trunk lid tied with string, dents and deep scrapes, bumper and rear end smashed. The windows and windshield were nothing but memories.

Highway 95 led me straight up the state and into Georgia, where I left Florida behind, sure I wouldn't be missed or welcomed back.

As the miles and hours passed, I took inventory.

I was an unmarried man or soon to be. In need of employment and income.

Right or wrong, I was also a murderer. And so far, I was living with that.

When the sun set, I got a motel room in Montgomery, Alabama. It was another white bag dinner followed by eleven hours of deadened sleep. The next morning, I found a Sears and bought new clothing: jeans and shirts and a pair of tan boots. Back on the road and heading west, I thumbed through the old contacts on my phone.

After playing catch up with my agent's secretary, my prior partner in crime in the world of movie making, Kevin Shutes, answered.

"I know that number. How are you?"

"Hey, Kevin. Good and you?"

"Starving, as always," he laughed. "Where are you?"

"On the road in the middle of nowhere."

"No longer in Florida, I hope? You got a lot of press for all the wrong reasons."

"I'm at least two states away, heading your way."

"Smart man."

"Rhonda told me about the offer. Is it still open?"

"Unfortunately, the cinematographer has been signed, but I can get you lead camera. You want it?"

The film in question was "Death Can be Murder" being produced at Blue Wave, same studio Rhonda worked for.

"Yes," I didn't hesitate.

"Good. Welcome back. With your notoriety, there'll be some back and forth, but I can cross those waters. What you need to do is get yourself here fast. Preproduction has started. You'll want in on all that. When can you get here?"

"I'm thinking I'm about three days away."

"Pierce? Get off the roads. Let me book you a fight."

"I'm good, thank you."

Why didn't I fly? Because it's a Buick. Get you anywhere.

***

By midmorning the following day, the drive was getting dangerous. It being early January, driving without a windshield turned me into a freezing hazard on wheels. Outside of Jackson, Mississippi, I found an auto glass shop and three hours later was back out on Highway 20.

To the hypnotic rhythm of windshield wipers on new glass, I

renewed my friendship with a long-departed serenity.

"Thank you," I told the stars above. They were up there, for certain, behind the rain clouds.

I was returning to the world of illusion, a place that had filled my heart and creative mind since my youth. Quite simply, I was headed for immersion.

Let the screenwriters and director build the story. All I wanted was to be inside the viewfinder, imagining and planning from the storyboards and discussions with the cinematographer. I was returning to the world of composition, working with a rich pallet of thematic colors. There would be choices of lighting and pace and rhythm and decisions about focus: I would again simply be the lens for a story. And for a while, away from the real world and all its unanswerable questions and pushes and pulls.

Chapter Thirty-Nine

Nineteen Weeks Later

"Grandpa?" Kazu floated in the pool.

"Yes?" I asked.

"I did a lot of really bad things."

"You were in some *really bad* situations."

"I keep looking back, no matter how hard I try not to."

"If it helps, think of your life as a car ride."

"What do you mean?"

What did I mean, indeed?

Kazu and I were enjoying a warm spring day, a blue sky above. I was sitting at the pool edge, good old Roadkill was sleeping at my side, occasionally pedaling through a dog's dream.

Beyond the swimming pool, in the field of young green wheat, Ali's eighty-foot ladder stood in the distance.

"A car ride?" he asked.

I turned to him.

Kazu was on top of his hand-built pirate ship, constructed with younger hands, a pontoon for balance attached by two by fours to the hull: a dog casket that he had convinced his mom to let him buy years before. Now it was too small to get his legs inside.

"Yes," I tried to explain. "With a simple choice. The mirrors or the windshield."

Kazu, Roadkill, and I were alone.

Bill, Ali, and Dan the Baby were off to town for seed and a thresher hitch part.

We had said our goodbyes in the driveway out front of the barn, Bill kidding me about the beat-up Buick that I had purchased from the rental company. After hugs and being asked to come back soon, Ali climbed up behind the wheel of her old long truck and they drove way.

"My life is a car ride?" Kazu's young voice was testing, pondering that.

"With a choice, yes. Look back or look forward."

From the back door of their farmhouse, Ali's stereo was playing wandering and colorful jazz, the melody both complex and barely staying on the rails of the composition.

"I like having a choice," Kazu said.

My cellphone played its alarm clock jingle. Reaching inside my pocket, I turned it off.

"It's time for me to go," I told Kazu. "Another season, another film. Walk me to my car?"

"You mean the wreck." He smirked.

I laughed with him.

Paddling with his hands, Kazu brought the boat to the pool's edge and clambered off it. Roadkill woke and looked up at him and went back to sleep.

We rounded the farmhouse and crossed the gravel of the driveway to my car.

Kazu put his arms around me. I kissed the top of his head, breathing the young fragrance of his hair.

"Grandpa?" he asked.

"Yes?"

"Thank you. I'm tilting my mirrors away."

The End

About the Author

Greg Jolley earned a Master of Arts in Writing from the University of San Francisco. He is the author of the suspense novels about the fictional Danser family. He lives in the Very Small town of Ormond Beach, Florida.

CPSIA information can be obtained
at www.ICGtesting.com
Printed in the USA
LVHW050802261221
707138LV00021B/2379

9 781088 000748